The

Newton Code

A Mystery Thriller

Liam Fialkov

https://www.facebook.com/liam.fialkov.77
liam_fialkov@outlook.com

2

Table of Contents

Chapter 1

Stop!!!

Where are you heading?

The message captured computer screens throughout the United States. The white, gothic font and an ornament of some sort were contrasted against a dark background. However, no one took the time to admire the carefully styled letters as they were busy absorbing their meaning: an unmistakable computer freeze.

"Damn it!" muttered a sweaty trader on the floor of the New York Stock Exchange as two of the computers he monitored while preparing for a transaction suddenly froze.

When he raised his head, he saw that every one of the hundreds of screens around the room displayed the same message.

In Chicago, that same second, a lawyer was about to hit "send" on his carefully drafted response to a plea bargain proposal when his screen froze with the same annoying message.

Throughout the country, frantic and annoyed users hurried to restart their computers and mobile devices—their lifeline connections to the world.

While their devices restarted, users were prepared to dismiss the odd interruption and delve back into their demanding tasks. Unfortunately, after their machines were once again functional, they displayed the same frozen screen with the irritating message, *"Stop!!! Where are you heading?"*

Frustrated users reached for their phones to call the computer guy or someone in the IT department who could help them get back to work.

But tech support personnel, if they were reached, could not provide any rescue from the crisis.

"We're checking," was the standard answer. "It looks like a virus," some of them volunteered the obvious.

All over the US, computers came to a standstill, rendering their owners helpless. The halt occurred exactly at 1:00 PM Eastern Time and affected all branches of the government as well as most of the private sector. It stalled traffic lights which

8

blinked yellow across the country, but didn't affect hospitals, airport control towers, and the rail transportation.

And then, all at once, exactly thirteen minutes after the start of the disturbance, everything went back to normal.

"What on earth was that?" was the question on everyone's mind.

By evening, it was mostly forgotten, except for a mention on the evening news, where most channels hosted technology specialists. However, the experts had to admit that they were unable to locate the source of the mysterious freeze. They noted that as far as computer security experts could tell, whatever it was left no trace in any code on any of the affected computers. Nor was there evidence of it having caused any damage to the data, programs, or operating systems. So, the experts gave a general explanation about computer viruses and other malware.

Hardly anybody paid attention to the ornament at the bottom right side of the screens. It displayed swirling carvings that decorated a golden, wooden box. Two wooden poles extended out of the box, one on each side as if to carry it, and sculptures of two winged seraphim were located on the hood.

Among those who paid attention to the decoration, only a few recognized what it was: a distinctive image of the Ark of the Covenant.

Chapter 2

Jerusalem, 1002 BC

Young Yerubaal didn't want to die.

Not even ten years old, he loved life. He loved strolling in the trails around his village, investigating the world as it woke up to a cool morning. He loved listening to the birds nesting in the oak, cedar, and olive trees. He loved sneaking at night, hiding in the darkness and secretly eavesdropping on the grown-ups as they chattered around the campfire. He listened as they discussed important matters and told stories of the ancient past. The child knew his tribal elders well enough to detect when their accounts slipped into exaggeration as they glorified victories in wars with their neighbors.

Although young, he already knew who his favorite girl was: charming Bat-Ashtoreth, with the long black hair, shiny and curly, and the large, cheerful brown eyes. Her graceful, agile movements reminded him of an antelope. More than anything, he loved listening to the chime of her laughter, and he knew that he wanted to wake up next to her in his adult life.

With his little brother, Ben-Reshef, he wandered around pathways, happily climbing large rocks and jumping from one rock to another. In several selected rocks, the tribesmen had carved large pits for winemaking, and during the grape harvest, they piled grapes in the pits, then pressed the grapes with their bare feet.

The first time Yerubaal had tried to drink wine, it had immediately made him dizzy and given him a terrible tummy ache. He'd sworn he'd never drink wine again.

There was one massive rock that they didn't carve or use for making wine. He was told that the rock, located on a threshing-floor owned by a man named Araunah, was sacred. Children were not allowed to play there.

Every once in a while, Yerubaal was present at ceremonies where he saw the tribal high priest slaughter animals, mostly lambs and partridges, on the big rock which they called "the drinking stone." It was a sacrifice to the gods, so he was told, and he wondered why they had to kill innocent animals in order to please the gods.

Yerubaal heard whispers alluding that in the distant past, his people used to sacrifice people as well, especially boys. Apprehensively, he asked his father if it was true, but his father asserted that, for many years, the Jebusites contented themselves and their gods with animal sacrifices.

However, the Jebusites now faced a formidable enemy that threatened their survival. Young Yerubaal knew that his tribe had fallen onto extremely hard times; but he never imagined that, of all people in his tribe, *he* would be required to pay the ultimate price.

One night, when most of the tribe lay sleeping, Yerubaal snuck by the campfire, where he saw his father sitting around the last crackling fire with their neighbor, Baal-Shalem. Ducking behind a nearby cluster of trees, Yerubaal listened to their hushed conversation.

"Hebron has fallen," Baal-Shalem said. "Their fortifications couldn't withstand the Hebrews' attack."

"The same is true for our allies at Lachish," Yerubaal's father said. "I'm afraid the Hebrews are gaining control over the entire land of Canaan."

"I am concerned for the future of our kingdom," Baal-Shalem confessed, shaking his head as he stared into the clay mug in his hands.

To Yerubaal's surprise and horror, his father nodded and said gravely, "It will not be long before King David sets his sights upon Jebus."

A few nights later, Yerubaal eavesdropped on his parents' conversation.

"I'm afraid," his mother whispered, clutching her elbows, "so afraid I can't fall asleep at night." She sat on a sheep's wool-blanket in their small brick home and bowed over her knees. Letting her hair slip over her shoulder, she hid her face from the dancing light of the hearth fire.

"You need not worry, Bat-Shahar," his father said, leaning forward to brush her dark hair out of her eyes. "You know that our town is well-fortified. It is located up on the mountain, which is why no one could conquer it in the past when other kingdoms fell one after the other."

"But now it's different," his mother said. "I've heard from Bat-Ashra, who heard from her husband, who is close to the high priest, that of all places, it is here that King David wants to establish his capital."

"Which is why we must pray and call upon our gods," his father replied. "We must offer sacrifices and hope that the gods, Baal and Ashtoreth, will support and protect us."

Indeed, on the following days, Yerubaal saw that the high priest and his clergy increased the rate of animal sacrifice, which soon became a daily occurrence.

Chapter 3

The phone rang.

Michael[1] glanced at his phone—on the table in front of him—and was surprised to see the name Stewart McPherson flashing across the screen.

"Stewart?" He didn't hide his surprise.

"That's me," said the veteran journalist in his familiar gravelly voice and somber tone—just like it had been five years earlier when they'd worked together. "How's life in the world of academia?"

"It pays the bills," Michael shrugged his shoulders, "and it's comfortable."

"But not too exciting, is it?" McPherson probed.

"True." Michael fiddled with his pen. He sensed this was more than a social call.

---

[1] Three of the protagonists, Michael, Melany, and McPherson, were introduced in my previous novel, *The Broadcast: A Mystery Thriller*.

While reading that novel is wholeheartedly recommended, it is not essential to the understanding and enjoyment of *The Newton Code*, which can be read as a standalone. – Liam Fialkov

"So, what are your plans for the upcoming summer?"

Michael hesitated for a brief moment. "You want me to go somewhere undercover?" Michael wasn't sure why he felt that his spine tingled.

"It's possible," McPherson answered in a tone much grimmer than his usual somber manner.

"Stewart," Michael said slowly, keeping his breathing controlled. "I thought I made it clear that I'm not spy material."

"You also made it clear that you're a person of high integrity, and someone I can count on."

"What is it this time?" Michael said with a hefty sigh, "What conspiracy are you trying to unearth?"

"I can't discuss it over the phone," McPherson said. "This time, the stakes could be much higher."

"Higher?" Michael asked, eyebrows rising. "Higher than spying on my employer?"

"Well, don't forget that you also got a great deal of satisfaction from being a part of that assignment," the journalist reminded him.

"Clearly, you're right," Michael admitted. He remembered how he got to play music in a rock band as part of that assignment, the same band of which he was still a member and with whom he played most weekends. He also met Melany, his wife, while on assignment for McPherson. "Is it something to do with the media world?"

"Probably not," McPherson replied in a grave tone of voice. "This time, I need you to help me prevent a global war."

Chapter 4

"Long time, no see." McPherson smiled. He shook Michael's hand warmly and tapped him on the shoulder with a broad hand.

About one week after McPherson's call, the two met at a café in Manhattan, not far from the university where Michael taught. Michael visited the place regularly. He thought it had a homey atmosphere, with its friendly staff, and wood-paneled walls decorated with landscape art of the French painter Paul Gauguin.

"Good to see you, Stewart," Michael replied. *Has it really been that long?* Michael wondered as he noticed the changes in his friend's face. McPherson's hair was now completely gray, the wrinkles in his face had deepened, and his skin color was pale. *He must be around sixty,* Michael thought to himself as he noted that McPherson's handshake was as firm as before, and he had the same penetrating yet kind eyes.

Michael regarded McPherson as a courageous fighter against corruption, worthy of being a role model.

After their phone call, Michael reflected on his previous collaboration with his esteemed colleague, about five years earlier. He realized that while he performed his task somewhat reluctantly, there were aspects of undercover work that he liked. Maybe it was the thrill of danger, or perhaps the idea of working on something grand and being chosen for the job by the renowned journalist. Now, though his initial response was that of hesitancy, he realized that he actually looked forward to some 'action' that would pull him out of his routine, comfortable life.

Michael liked his life. He did. He was blessed to have found Melany, his true love, blessed for the life they had built together and for their daughter, Linda. Blessed to have found a career he was passionate about, teaching investigative journalism. Michael was grateful to have found his biological mom after years of yearning, and he didn't forget McPherson's help in tracking her. He treasured his friends and the rock 'n' roll band in which he played lead guitar on weekends.

But every now and then, something about his comfortable lifestyle felt off. Wrong, somehow, or incomplete. Like there was a hole in his life, but he didn't know how to fill it. So, he'd recognized that McPherson's call had perhaps come at an opportune time, and he'd eagerly awaited their meeting.

"You sounded mysterious," Michael said. They sat at a corner table at a late morning hour. Apart from the elderly couple sitting at a table by the window and the occasional customer grabbing a coffee-to-go, the spacious café was empty.

"Do you remember our last collaboration?" McPherson asked.

"How can I forget?" Michael replied. "Sometimes, I wonder where I would be if you hadn't recruited me for that spying mission."

The waitress came by, and McPherson ordered an espresso and a croissant.

"I'll have what he is having," Michael said.

The waitress wrote their order and clicked away on her heels.

"You probably remember," McPherson said, "that I didn't ask you to approach anyone directly, but devised a way by which you would attract Lindsey's attention so that he would be the one to approach you."

"I remember," Michael concealed his smile. "I had to play the guitar. I think that's why I accepted the assignment."

"I'm asking you to proceed in a similar manner," McPherson said.

"You want me to play the guitar?"

"Well, not this time. But first," McPherson cleared his throat, "I want to be clear that I'm reaching out to you because it's something that I couldn't do on my own. I'm too recognizable."

Michael let out a fond chuckle in response to McPherson's allusion to his fame, as footsteps approached. The clicking of heels on wood was soon followed by their waitress, who set their order on the low table in front of them before clip-clopping away.

"What do you want me to do?" Michael asked, meeting McPherson's eyes.

"I want you to go online," McPherson said, sipping his coffee with a knowing gleam in his eyes, as if he knew every doubtful thought trekking across Michael's mind.

"Online?" Though Michael tried, he couldn't see the barest hint of amusement on McPherson's face.

"Not just online, but to specific websites—I'll give you the URLs—where certain people meet and exchange information.

22

Try to sound interested in their theories, learn all you can about their agenda, and wait until *they* approach you."

"Who are those certain people?" Michael asked, taking a bite of his croissant.

"A group that admires Sir Isaac Newton."

"Newton?" Michael's eyes widened. "The seventeenth-century scientist?"

"Yes," McPherson said and fixed him with a stern glare. "From now on, we have to be utterly discreet about this mission."

"Fine," Michael said, realizing that he was talking somewhat loudly.

"What do you know about Sir Isaac Newton?" McPherson asked, and nibbled on his croissant.

"Not a whole lot," Michael admitted. "I know that he was one of the greatest scientists of all time. He pioneered the field of calculus, and of course, he is known for developing the theory of gravity."

"And much more," McPherson said. "He also laid the foundations for classical mechanics as well as established the field of optics. He was instrumental in founding the laws of motion, and he calculated the tides, the trajectories of comets, the speed of sound, and much, much more."

"Quite a capable guy," Michael nodded.

"Even with all of his recognized achievements," McPherson continued, "there's a lot about Newton that's not widely known by, and perhaps even hidden from, the general public."

"Like what?" Michael slid his chair closer to the table and leaned forward.

"Newton dedicated much of his time and energy to alchemy, metaphysics, and unorthodox biblical theories."

"Sounds a bit strange." Michael's eyebrows furrowed as he considered the new information. "I wasn't aware of that."

"I have a list of online resources for you to study and a group you should try to mingle with. You'll have to convince them that you're genuine. Don't be surprised if they're suspicious toward you, at least in the beginning. Now the important part which, at the moment, is the focus of this unofficial investigation," McPherson examined Michael with a piercing look. "You need to learn Newton's theories regarding the first Jewish temple in Jerusalem."

"The first Jewish temple?"

"There were two temples built on the exact same spot in Jerusalem. Both were destroyed," McPherson said. "The first one is also known as the Temple of Solomon, since it was built by King Solomon. There is plenty of information about it in the Old Testament, as well as on the internet."

"So, is this a Jewish group?" Michael wondered.

"Not at all," McPherson replied. "They are devout Christians."

"It sounds interesting," Michael scratches his head, "but also odd. I mean, I had no idea that Newton wrote anything about the ancient temple."

"He wrote a lot," McPherson said. "He studied the temple compulsively, and these writings don't always appear where you'd expect to find them."

McPherson pulled a small notebook and a pen out of his pocket and scribbled something onto a page. He tore out the paper, folded it, and handed it over to Michael, who smiled at the ritualistic gesture. Michael unfolded the paper, curious at what it was that McPherson clearly attempted to emphasize. It was just a number: 2520.

"Find out what you can about this number," McPherson said in a somber tone of voice.

"I'll do my best," Michael promised. "And by the way, is Irene helping you with your project? She's a computer genius, right?"

Michael was one of the selected few who'd been invited to McPherson's small and modest wedding to Irene, his second wife.

"She sure is," McPherson confirmed, his smile softening at the question. "Irene's on a sabbatical, so she's helping me on some projects, because, as you know, my computer skills are somewhat limited."

"I'm due for a sabbatical in the upcoming school year," Michael said as he finished his coffee. "I'm looking forward to having time for myself."

"I'm sensing you might need a break from teaching," McPherson smirked.

"You're right. I've been questioning many things lately."

As they stood and prepared to leave, McPherson had one last thing to emphasize. "Be extremely cautious. These people are religious fanatics who are willing to bring on a world war. You must not trigger their suspicion."

Chapter 5

"Hi, honey." Melany, dressed in her nightgown, shuffled into his home office. She rubbed her eyes, yawning. "Is everything all right?"

Michael glanced at the clock on the wall and saw that it was past 3:00 AM.

"I noticed that you've been going to bed very late," she stated the obvious. "You also seem quite preoccupied recently. What's going on?"

He turned away from the computer and looked at her. Even in the minimal light in the small room, he couldn't help but adore her beauty. For a moment, he recalled how he'd been drawn to her when they first met. There was something about her that he'd never felt with any girl he'd met before. A sweetness that made him want to kiss her right there and then. That hasn't changed over the years, he now realized. Unwilling to breach her father's trust in him, he hadn't approached her for several months. Eventually, it was Melany who'd made the first move when she'd asked him out.

"It is strange, Lanie," he said pensively, "but there is one thing that I don't know if we'd ever discussed, at least not in a profound way."

"What is it?" She sank into the armchair in front of him and waited.

"God."

"God?" Her eyes widened a touch.

"Yes," he said. "I'm studying the issue." He smiled, knowing his words deserved an explanation.

She observed him, his athletic body erect in his simple computer chair with his wavy black hair over his forehead. His eyes glowed in the dim room. She briefly recalled the first time she'd seen Michael and how she thought that he'd been sculpted like a statue of a Greek god. *That hasn't changed much,* she thought to herself.

She wondered about the unexpected topic. "I thought we were atheists."

Michael contemplated her words.

"Well, I know I am an atheist," she added.

"But perhaps we should give the matter another thought," he said. "As far as I know, some of the world's greatest thinkers considered themselves believers, like Einstein and Newton."

28

"Especially Newton," she asserted.

He was surprised. "Why *especially* Newton?"

"I once read," she said, "that in addition to science, he held a deep interest in the Christian scriptures."

"The Christian and the Jewish scriptures," Michael corrected.

"But why now?" she asked. "What's triggered your sudden interest in God?"

"Stewart McPherson."

"McPherson?" she echoed in surprise. "I haven't heard from him in ages. Is he still in town?"

"I met him in a downtown café," Michael said. "He keeps his old office in Manhattan."

"Well, we haven't moved much either."

"We will," he said. He knew Melany wanted to leave Brooklyn and buy a home in the country. He liked the idea, too, but delayed the move, dreading a long daily commute. "I'll tell you what's going on, but it must remain a secret. Please don't discuss this with anybody."

"Okay."

Michael knew for certain that he could trust her word. "Stewart approached me a couple of weeks ago, and asked me to join him in an investigation. Apparently, there's a cult, a very sophisticated, well-organized, and well-funded group, that McPherson suspects is planning something very sinister."

"How sinister?"

"They may be striving to bring on a world war."

"A world war? Why? Between whom?"

"Probably Christians against Muslims. They want to create the conditions for the second coming of Jesus Christ."

"Oh, my God," she exclaimed, then yawned. "Hun, this is all very fascinating and scary, but I have to be in court early in the morning. Let's continue tomorrow."

"I'll be here," Michael promised.

She got up and embraced him. As she aimed for the door, she glanced at his computer screen.

"What is that, Hun?" She pointed to the computer.

"It's Hebrew script," he said. "Well, actually, it's not even Hebrew, but Aramaic, an ancient language which nobody speaks anymore."

She examined the writing:

מְנֵא מְנֵא, תְּקֵל וּפַרְסִין

"What does it mean?" she asked.

"Here," he said, smiling, "I'll show you the English version." He scrolled down on the page, which now displayed:

"MENE MENE, TEKEL, UPHARSIN."

"It's called 'the Writing on the Wall,' from the biblical Book of Daniel, chapter five," Michael explained. "It's supposed to have a hidden meaning."

"I see," she said, covering her mouth with her hand as she yawned. "I'm sleepy, I'm going back to bed now, I think you could use some sleep too."

She left the room.

Michael watched her as she walked away. He loved her. He knew she was the love of his life. He adored her beauty and the way she went out of her way to help other people when they were in distress, or how she donated generously to homeless people she walked by on the street. He also highly valued the wisdom and insights she offered during his moments of doubt and confusion.

However, he couldn't ignore the nagging drops of discontent that trickled into his mind from time to time. It wasn't that he'd stopped loving her; it was just that it all became mundane. They were both so busy with their work and other responsibilities that it seemed like they'd started treating each other as partners more than lovers, like they were merely allies in some undefined mission they called life. Nothing seemed wrong, but they had fallen into some patterns that were growing monotonous. Even their sex, now that he considered it, though enjoyable, had become a routine for them.

There were hardly any romantic surprises that had once been a prominent aspect of their relationship. Something wasn't the same. Was this the expected result of marriage? Were they taking each other for granted?"

It can't be a mid-life crisis; I'm only thirty-two.

Michael swiveled his chair around to look at the computer: *MENE MENE, TEKEL, UPHARSIN.* The Writing on the Wall.

Was there anything about that message that he was missing?

Chapter 6

"Hun," Melany, wearing striped pajamas, entered his office after tucking little Linda in bed. "What did you mean the other day when you said we never discussed God?"

Michael looked at her affectionately. He loved it when they discussed profound questions, as there was much more than the subject matter in those conversations. They met each other, looked into each other's eyes as they communicated soul to soul, and together delved deeply into subtle worlds, learning and growing as one. Sadly, it had been quite some time since their last profound discussion.

He leaned to the right, reaching into his cabinet and pulled out a thick, weathered, leather-bound book. "I found this book a few days ago in a used bookstore. It's not the first edition, but it's quite old. Believe it or not, it might be the most important book in the history of modern science. It's called *Mathematical Principles of Natural Philosophy*, and it was written about three hundred years ago by Sir Isaac Newton."

"Newton again?" Melany noted, as her brown eyes lit up with interest.

"Let me read to you what Newton says about God in this *scientific* book." Michael opened the book into a page marked with a piece of paper, and read aloud:

"The true God is a living, intelligent, and powerful Being. He is eternal and infinite, omnipotent and omniscient; that is, His duration reaches from eternity to eternity; his presence from infinity to infinity; he governs all things, and knows all things that are or can be done."

Michael glanced at Melany, to make sure she was following him, then continued:

"He endures forever, and is everywhere present; and by existing always and everywhere, he constitutes duration and space. Since every particle of space is always, and every indivisible moment of duration is everywhere, certainly the Maker and Lord of all things cannot be never and nowhere."

Michael gently closed the book and looked at her.

"Well, truly interesting," Melany commented, "especially coming from such a genius as Newton, and in a scientific book. It certainly shows that he was a believer."

"Indeed," Michael said, "Newton was a devout Christian."

34

"Still," she said, her bright gaze fixed on his. "Those passages are not enough to convince me to go to church anytime soon."

"I don't think Newton himself had spent much time in church," Michael said. "He didn't follow the mainstream dogma of the Church of England and was somewhat of a heretic in that he didn't accept the idea of the Holy Trinity. It is well-known that he'd spent much time searching for what is called the *prisca sapientia*."

"What's that?" Melany asked.

"The lost pure knowledge," Michael answered. "Interestingly, Newton was convinced that ancient civilizations possessed that core knowledge which they consciously concealed, and his brilliant findings were not discoveries but merely *re*-discoveries."

Melany contemplated for a while.

Michael observed how she furrowed her eyebrows and looked somewhere behind him. He loved looking at her. After all those years, he still perceived a touch of a young girl's appearance in her pretty face.

Finally, she asked, "Did Newton find that pure knowledge?"

"We don't know," Michael replied. "You see, if he had, he wasn't the type of person who would go around telling the world about it. It's more likely that he would have kept it to himself or perhaps hidden it within his other papers." Michael paused and then leaned to his right to put the book back on the cabinet. "You know, Newton discovered that white light was composed of the colors of the rainbow. In that respect, you could say that he saw the light."

"There is one major thing that deserves an explanation," Melany said and locked his gaze with hers.

"What?"

"What's this sudden interest in old Isaac Newton? Is it related to McPherson?"

Michael took a deep breath and nodded. "Yes."

"He was like a mentor to you," Melany said.

"And a role model," Michael added. "Remember the cult I told you about?"

"Yes," she said. "They want to bring on a world war."

"That's right. Well, the same cult is also obsessed with Newton and—"

"You're not going undercover again, are you?" Melany frowned.

"At this point, I'm just researching the topic," Michael said.

36

Chapter 7

Jerusalem, 1002 BC

The ominous news spread rapidly. Despite fortified defense barriers and animal sacrifices, King David's soldiers succeeded in conquering the Jebusites' front lines. They inflicted heavy losses upon the Jebusites and cut off Jebus from its primary water source in the Gihon creek. The siege intensified, and the tribe was forced to make do with the limited water reservoirs which they maintained for such a disastrous hour. They also collected water from occasional rains.

The Jebusites believed all was not lost, as they still controlled the higher, most fortified walls. If they could only withstand the siege without starving, maybe the Hebrews would give up and let them be? Perhaps an unexpected ally would come to their aid, or their ferocious war goddess, Anat, would intervene? Or maybe the Hebrews would choose to live side by side, conducting commerce with the Jebusites so both sides would benefit?

But then, King David's soldiers conquered the Zion fortress and its adjacent fortified line. The Jebusites retreated up the mountain to Araunah's threshing floor and formed a new line of defense next to the massive rock—*the drinking stone*. They knew that the battle had been decided; they just didn't know what would happen to them. Would King David have mercy on their lives, or would his soldiers slaughter them?

A day passed. It looked like the Hebrew soldiers were in no hurry to attack, or perhaps they thought that the Jebusites would be overcome by despair and surrender. They may have wanted to avoid further casualties on their side, or they just took their time, planning their next offensive move.

For the Jebusites, the wait was nerve-wracking. Rumor in the Jebusite camp had it that the Hebrews were waiting for the king's decision, and he consulted with a prophet named Gad the Seer.

***

That night, Yerubaal's family, like the rest of the tribe, camped outside, not far from the homes they were forced to leave behind.

Yerubaal's father went to an urgent meeting summoned by the tribe's high priest. Upon his return, he spoke in furious whispers to Yerubaal's mother, who clasped a hand over her mouth and doubled over as he finished. He then strode toward Yerubaal to deliver the news.

"We were greatly honored," he said, not sounding at all like one who had been awarded a great honor. Rather, he sounded deeply saddened and distressed. His dark gaze was averted as he added in a barely audible mutter, "Greatly honored, greatly honored."

But Yerubaal's mother, behind him, let out a terrible wail and shot forward, running to Yerubaal and collecting him into a bone-crushing hug. Her tears drenched his face, so he disentangled himself from her.

"What? What happened?" The child asked, glancing between them.

"Greatly honored," his father continued to mumble, while his shoulders sagged in defeat. He turned his gaze toward the dark mountains as if waiting for some unidentified rescue to appear out of nowhere.

Yerubaal couldn't remember when his father wouldn't look at him directly.

"Oh, my sweet baby," his mom wailed. While still weeping, she looked into his eyes. "You know that we're in a tough situation, sweetie. I wouldn't exaggerate if I said a desperate situation."

Fear gripped the boy. He sensed that a dreadful thing was about to happen, not necessarily to the tribe as a whole, but to him personally.

"The high priest," his mother continued, her tears glistening in the dim light of their dying fire. "He is the one who named you, Yerubaal."

"He chose you," his father said in a croaky voice when it appeared he recovered some of his composure.

"Chose me? For what?" The boy asked, uncontrolled shivering overtaking him.

"The high priest," his mother said, "has prayed to Baal, after whom you are named. The message he received from the god was clear: Baal wants *you* in exchange for saving Jebus, and thus, we have to sacrifice you…"

"Sacrifice?" Yerubaal's heart pounded. "But why?"

"It's the will of the gods," his father said. "It's the only way that our tribe will survive."

40

Yerubaal didn't want to hear any more. He ran fast, escaping his parents and headed toward the mountain.

"Let him go," his father told his mother. "He'll come back."

Chapter 8

"Tell me more about Newton," Melany asked.

On a Sunday afternoon, Michael was driving their Toyota Prius, heading back to their apartment in Brooklyn. Melany sat next to him and five-year-old Linda slept in the back seat, exhausted after a birthday party in Scarsdale.

Michael took a deep breath, wondering which angle he should take. "Well, his father died a few months before he was born."

Melany contemplated his answer, wondering if Michael, who grew up as an adopted child, felt a kinship with Newton.

"He was born on Christmas Eve, sometime in the seventeenth century," Michael added. "He was probably premature, and since he looked so frail, his mother had put him in the attic to die alone. She didn't believe he would survive the freezing winter night. However, Baby Isaac cried and screamed so loudly that his mother realized he was much stronger than she thought, and he should be given a chance to survive. So, she brought him to a warm room and fed him.

According to a local English folk tale, a baby born without a father on Christmas Eve is destined for greatness and possesses special holiness."

"Sounds like he was off to a rough start," Melany commented.

"True," Michael agreed, "and that's how his early life continued after his mother married a local priest who didn't like him."

"But hun," Melany said, "I want to hear about why *you* are spending nights learning about him. I mean, I know that you're working with McPherson on that, but I still don't get why both of you are doing it."

"Okay," Michael said while maneuvering the car between busy lanes. "It's quite bizarre, but Newton, the great mathematician, the inventor of calculus and numerous other pioneering works, spent more time studying theology and alchemy than on science."

"That's really weird," Melany said, "and I'd assume that the cult you've mentioned the other night is more interested in that aspect of Newton's work."

"Yes," Michael said. "When studying the Old Testament, Newton, who was fluent in Latin and ancient Hebrew, learned that *God* dictated the exact measurements of the temple in

Jerusalem, the one built by King Solomon. God also dictated the measurements of the Ark of the Covenant. Of course, those measurements were not dictated in feet and inches, rather in the old Hebrew cubits. Still, Newton concluded that since the creator of the world is also the designer of the temple and Ark, then there must be a correlation between those measurements and the dimensions of our universe."

Melany shook her head. "Wow."

"Yep," Michael said. "He saw the temple and the surrounding courtyard as a model of our solar system. The altar, located in the center, represented the sun."

"If I heard that this kind of thinking came from some insignificant theologian or some outcast cult, I would find it somewhat understandable," Melany said, "but when it comes from one of the greatest minds in history, it sure sounds strange."

"There's another option," Michael said, as he took a right turn towards Brooklyn.

"What?"

"Well, I think that we shouldn't completely close our minds to the possibility that there is something to his assumptions."

"Hun?" Melany sounded concerned. "Are you serious? A relationship between a temple that had been destroyed centuries ago and the universe? That just doesn't make sense."

"It's quite a stretch," Michael agreed. "I just think that since we're talking about Newton, we shouldn't reject the whole notion right off the bat, but try to understand what he meant."

"One more thing," Melany said. "The other night, when I entered your office, there was a strange verse on your computer screen.

"That's right," Michael said, "*Mene Mene, Tekel, Upharsin.*"

"You never told me what it means, and how it may connect to Newton," she said.

"Well," Michael said, "you would have to read that chapter in the Book of Daniel; it's pretty short. As for Newton, he was especially interested in old biblical prophecies, and he even wrote a book titled *Observations Upon the Prophecies of Daniel, and the Apocalypse of St. John.* So, I think that to understand Newton better, I have to familiarize myself with those old prophecies."

"Did you read that book?" she inquired.

"Not thoroughly," he admitted. "I haven't had time, and it's quite ambiguous. But in a different book, I read about the hidden meaning of *Mene Mene, Tekel, Upharsin,* which could explain why Newton was so interested in it."

Melany glanced at the back seat to make sure Linda was still sleeping. "So, what is the hidden meaning?"

"It's a number," Michael responded. "Those words could represent monetary values. I don't remember the exact math, but the total number comes to 2520."

"2520?" Melany's eyes widened. "What's so special about that number?"

"At this point," Michael said, "I don't know enough to answer that question; but, apparently, it's some kind of a magic number hidden in various ways throughout the Bible, both Old and New Testaments. It could represent distances, times, or both. For instance, God created the world in seven days; each day, the earth revolves 360 degrees. Seven times 360 equals 2520, so on the first week of creation, the earth rotated 2520 degrees."

Michael pulled into the parking lot of their apartment building and stopped the car.

"Interestingly," Michael added, "while Newton spent a great deal of time studying prophecies and focusing on the Books of Daniel and Revelation, as of yet, I've not found that he even mentioned 2520. So, apparently, this angle comes from other sources."

"What sources?"

"Well, Newton was not the only theologian who looked for hidden messages in the Bible."

"So, you are studying other theologians as well?"

"I'm concentrating on Newton because he's the focus of the cult. There are several scholars who studied Newton's work, and they agree that he wasn't too keen on sharing information. He could have kept certain information hidden, and that could include 2520."

"You know, honey," Melany said with tender concern, "I'm worried this stuff is going to mess with your head."

"I don't think you need to worry about me," Michael said "For now, it's just research."

Michael turned off the engine. He opened the car's back door, lifted his sleeping daughter from the back seat, draped her against his shoulder, and proceeded toward their apartment. Melany followed him after collecting their bags and Linda's clothes and toys.

Chapter 9

For he (Abraham) was looking forward to the city with foundations,
whose architect and builder is God.

   - ***New Testament, Hebrews 11***

When Michael examined the different web sites that
McPherson sent him, he realized that most of them were old,
amateurish, and rarely used.

However, one site drew his attention with its professional
layout and tasteful, thoughtful design.

The site, which was peculiarly named *His Time*, was built
to look like Solomon's temple's floor plan. It contained
several "chambers," dedicated to various forums that were
open to the public. The exception was the Holy of Holies,
which required a password.

One chamber was a forum dedicated to the interpretations
of biblical prophecies, especially from the Book of Revelation
and the Book of Daniel. In another chamber, participants
discussed Newton's scientific breakthroughs, comparing them

to Einstein's and analyzing complex mathematical formulae. Another chamber was dedicated to women's issues throughout the centuries. Michael was surprised to find a somewhat hidden chamber where participants discussed weapons and focused on explosives and ways to detonate and bring down large structures.

Sitting comfortably at the computer in his home office and lurking within the website's chambers, Michael used the alias *Angel Mikhael*. That way he kept a similar scheme of nomenclature as other participants, like *Saint Paulus, Saint Miriam, Apostle Yohanan,* and *The Ark Bishop.*

After lurking for a couple of weeks, he decided to make his presence known. So, every once in a while, he asked questions and contributed to discussions.

He found that while some participants were clearly novices, like him, others were knowledgeable, and a few were experts in everything that had to do with Newton, the Temple of Solomon, and old prophecies.

One time, he participated in a live forum hosted by a person identified as *Saint Miriam.* Michael liked her forums because they were informative and used clear language, without drifting into a pretentious jargon and unfamiliar terminology. This forum took place in a most central area of the temple's floor plan, right outside the Holy of Holies.

Saint Miriam took the time to patiently explain the significance and importance of the temple's location. She cited from a Hebrew scripture called the Babylonian Talmud:

> *The world is like a human eyeball. The white of the eye is the ocean surrounding the world, the iris is this continent, the pupil is Jerusalem, And the image in the pupil is the Holy Temple.*

Michael asked permission to pose a question, and, when granted, he typed.

Angel Mikhael: "I understand that we have the measurements of Solomon's temple, which are described in detail in the Bible and in Newton's writings. However, I find it hard to see how these measurements are related to the universe or our solar system."

Saint Miriam: "Thank you for a truly valuable question. I suggest that, to get an answer to such a profound inquiry, you talk directly to the *Ark Bishop*. You can find him in the Holy of Holies."

50

Angel Mikhael: "I don't have access to the Holy of Holies."

Saint Miriam: "You'll have to figure it out. Or you could wait, and he might contact you."

Angel Mikhael: "Thank you."

Saint Miriam: "Last thing for today, The *Ark Bishop* has announced that we are getting close to the momentous day. Very soon, those who are truly committed to the cause will be called to the land. The time for action is coming."

Chapter 10

Stop!!!

Where are you heading?

Are you following in the path of the lord?

"Oh, not again!" A frantic sigh echoed throughout the country as millions of computer users found themselves facing another freeze.

"Oh, no!" said drivers as traffic lights turned to blinking yellow, promising long traffic jams.

Once again, the computer screens displayed the message in a pleasant, well-designed way, ornamented as before with the Ark of the Covenant. Frustrated users were in no mood to appreciate it. Like the previous event, the halt affected all the government branches and most of the private sector. It didn't affect hospitals, control towers in airports, train lines, and anything that had to do with emergency life support.

This time, however, the halt was not limited to the United States. It included Canada, most Western European countries, and Israel. It didn't include China, Russia, Iran, and North Korea, which could have pointed to intervention by a foreign country.

The halt, which started at 1:00 PM Eastern Time, lasted exactly thirteen minutes before it was lifted and everything returned to normal.

"What on earth was that?" The question was on everyone's mind.

***

"The US government formed a special task force to look into the severe computer freezes that recently impacted our country." Nancy Whitefield, the TXB TV network's anchorwoman, read her lines from the teleprompter. "TXB News has learned," she continued with a somber facial expression, "that we are consulting with our closest and most trusted allies worldwide." Not even thirty years old and already a seasoned broadcaster, she looked directly at the camera and nodded toward her viewers. "With the help of our technical commentator, Mr. Alan Baker, we'll try to get a further understanding of this troubling matter." The anchorwoman then turned to her right. "Good evening, Mr. Baker."

"Good evening Nancy," Alan Baker said. "It is outrageous!" He went straight into the monologue he'd prepared. "Somebody is shutting us down, and we don't have a clue as to who's behind it!"

"I'm sure," Nancy Whitfield said, "that the authorities are doing their best to get to the bottom of this."

"Yes," responded the commentator, pounding his fists against the table, "and in the meantime, our country is completely vulnerable and exposed to a foreign attack!"

"And what do you think of the suggested religious connotation which the messages imply?" The anchorwoman asked.

"I think it's completely irrelevant," answered the commentator, his face turning red. "The fact is that somebody—a person, a group, or a country—has the means of bringing this country to its knees, and we are groping in the dark. Do you realize that they could drag us back to the Stone Age without firing one bullet?"

"Do you have any theory as to who is behind these computer freezes?" Nancy Whitfield inquired.

54

Alan Baker took a deep breath and tried to relax. "In my opinion, it could be one of two options, either the perpetrators have given our government an ultimatum—like a demand to release jailed terrorists, or they are merely testing their capabilities. Whichever it is, I think that the authorities should place this issue at the top of their list of priorities."

"I'm sure they do," the anchorwoman smiled at her guest, "and thank you, Alan, for coming to our studio."

Chapter 11

"*Ark Bishop*, hah?" Stewart McPherson frowned.

"That's what she said," Michael confirmed and cited, "the *Ark Bishop* has announced that we are getting close to the momentous day." Michael leaned back into his velvet-lined chair. He sat in McPherson's spacious office in Manhattan on the other side of the journalist's massive, cherry-wood desk.

McPherson pushed his chair backward and rose from his seat. A tall man, it took him just two confident strides to get to the cabinet behind him. "Coffee?" he asked as he reached the coffee machine.

"No, thanks."

McPherson started pacing around the room and seemed wrapped in thoughts.

"Hmm," he mumbled. "The dots are starting to connect."

Michael wasn't sure whether he was talking to him or to himself.

McPherson sat back in his chair without the coffee. "I've been following this man for some time regarding another investigation," McPherson said, rubbing his unshaven jaw. "Now, when you mentioned the name *Bishop*, I suddenly realized that it's the same man. My assumption is that the two matters are not separate from one another."

"I thought," Michael said, "that *Ark Bishop* is a nickname."

"You may be right, but I don't think so," McPherson said, scratching a white eyebrow as he gazed out of a floor-to-ceiling window. "If I'm correct, we are facing a man named *Charles Bishop*."

"Sounds interesting." Michael leaned forward, his interest piqued.

"Let me tell you about Charles Bishop," McPherson said. "He was a soldier in the American army in Afghanistan and then Iraq. A few days before his scheduled return home, the regiment he commanded stumbled upon an ambush, carefully planned by Shi'a, guerilla fighters. In the ensuing battle, Bishop demonstrated remarkable bravery. Under intense enemy fire, he succeeded in saving almost all of his men. He was severely injured, and for a few days, the army doctors didn't know if he would make it. He survived, though a bullet lodged in his spine rendered him paralyzed and unable to move his legs, so he's now confined to a wheelchair. For his courage, sacrifice, and composure under fire, he received the

Presidential Medal of Honor, as well as the Purple Heart medal."

"Sad," Michael said with a heavy sigh. "I don't think that any medal could compensate for being disabled for the rest of your life."

"Anyway," McPherson said, holding Michael's gaze for a long second before continuing. "Charles Bishop's spirit remained strong. He'd found solace in religion, and encouraged by his pastor, he became a devout Christian.

"He went back to school and studied computer programming. After just two years of studying, he left the university and founded a start-up company that specialized in digital security systems, antivirus, firewall, and the like. Within just five years, he sold his company for a huge profit, estimated at one-point-three billion dollars. He purchased a huge ranch in a remote location in Washington State, where he is living today.

"I don't know much about what's going on inside the ranch. According to my local source, the grounds are protected by electrified barbed wire, cameras, and possibly armed guards. Apparently, he's hiding something, otherwise, what's all this defense for?"

"Stewart," Michael asked, "are you convinced that Charles Bishop is the *Ark Bishop*?"

"I am," McPherson answered, "but not just that. My investigation of him was regarding a completely different matter. Now I'm starting to see that the two issues are related. Perhaps, I should have seen the connection earlier."

"So, what's the other issue?" Michael asked.

"Remember the recent strange computer freezes that practically crippled the country?" McPherson asked.

"Of course," Michael responded. "It affected the offices at my university."

"Well," McPherson said, toying with a pen on his desk. "I looked into the matter because I thought that it was a bigger story than met the eye, and, after talking to a few of my contacts, I discovered that our authorities didn't have a clue.

"At first, it seemed like a prank or an act of defiance committed by college students. Later, I examined the possibility of a foreign government's involvement. When I began to suspect that Charles Bishop was behind it, I didn't have a lot to base my suspicion on. It was more of a hunch, though you know, I've been in this business many years, and I've learned to trust my intuition.

"I inferred it was Bishop because he had the means and the knowledge to pull such a thing off, and because of the religious undertone.

"At that point, I didn't know the purpose of those acts. But now, as I'm talking to you, I'm starting to see the bigger picture."

"I sure don't see the bigger picture," Michael said. He couldn't help but notice how bright McPherson's eyes were. The old man was probably enjoying showing off his smarts.

"For example," McPherson said, "both computer failures happened at exactly 1:00 PM Eastern Time and lasted exactly thirteen minutes.

"So?"

"Think about it, Michael," McPherson urged him. "By now you know enough to figure out why it was those specific times."

"Stewart," Michael let out an exasperated sigh and crossed his arms, falling back into his plush chair. He had the distinct impression that McPherson was intentionally keeping him one step behind. "I don't have the faintest idea."

"Well," McPherson said, "the time was 1:00 PM, which could be looked upon as twelve hours plus sixty minutes. So, let's look at it simply as 1260.

"I don't see where you're going with this," Michael said, irritated, as he noticed McPherson's face displaying a playful grin.

"The freeze lasted for thirteen minutes," McPherson continued. "Again, this could be looked at as twelve minutes and sixty seconds. One more time we get 1260."

"And?" Michael asked.

"Michael," McPherson smiled affectionately at him, "we got 1260 twice. How much is 1260 times two?"

"2520?" Michael's irritation dissipated as he sensed a tingling all along his skin.

"Exactly," McPherson said, his knowing eyes crinkling around the edges. "If we're investigating these guys, we have to learn to think like them. According to their point of view, these symbols might mean that they are aligning their mission with the right prophecy and path."

Chapter 12

Yerubaal spent the night in a cave where he used to play with his brother. He didn't close his eyes the whole night, wondering if the god Baal, or another deity from the land of Canaan, would come to his aid. When he heard nothing from the gods, his mind filled with thoughts of heresy. *Do the gods really exist? I have never really seen them. And if they exist, maybe they are less powerful than the god of the Hebrews?*

Yerubaal recalled an odd thing his father had said. When Yerubaal had asked him if the Hebrews believe in the same gods as the Jebusites, his father had replied that the Hebrews only had one god. "Not like us," his father had elaborated. "We have Baal and Ashtoreth, we have El and Oshra, we have Dagon, Sea, Moon, Death, and all the others, and of course we have Anat, the goddess of war, who is helping us win our battles against our enemies."

The boy considered running away, *but where?* The Hebrew soldiers might catch him, and then, they would kill him. He never went anywhere beyond the surrounding mountains, and his world was confined to his native village.

Shortly after dawn, he made his way back to his family—back to the only home he'd known. He felt as if he walked against his will, not in control of his feet, which dragged him toward his demise. They ate breakfast in silence, noting that the Hebrew soldiers were in no hurry to start their final assault. Maybe the prayers and sacrifices helped? Perhaps they would not have to sacrifice Yerubaal?

When the sun reached its highest point in the sky, the blare of a trumpet echoing from the distant Hebrew camp told the Jebusites the hour had arrived. It was time. Time to show the king and his soldiers that the Jebusites were a proud people and fearless warriors—they were not going to die without a fight. Yerubaal watched his father strap on his freshly-sharpened sword and heavy armor, and join the tribesmen who prepared to face their enemy. The sun's golden rays gilded the Jebusites' bronze armor that symbols of the war goddess Anat were engraved on their breastplates and wrist cuffs. Although vastly outnumbered, they kept a glimmer of hope that the gods will intervene and turn the battle into a glorious victory for the Jebusites—a triumph that would be remembered around the campfires for generations.

The fighting had not yet begun, but the warriors were already sweating inside their cumbersome armor outfits.

Surprisingly, only one of King David's soldiers was seen approaching them. He carried and waved a white flag that had an unrecognized symbol painted on.

The Jebusite archers raised their weapons and aimed their arrows, preparing to meet the delegate with a lethal shower; but the high priest signaled them to lower their arches.

"We'd better listen to what he has to say," he said.

The delegate walked toward the Jebusites and stopped about twenty cubits from them. Shiny armor covered most of his body, but left his head and face exposed and unprotected. Yerubaal noted that he didn't look particularly threatening; instead, he looked like the Jebusite grown-ups. "The great King David, glorified by God for eternity!" the delegate declared in the Canaan's local language, "requests a meeting with Araunah!"

Araunah was the richest man of all Jebusites, important among the tribe, and ranking higher in authority than

64

Yerubaal's parents. The boy thought him mean and arrogant. Regardless, it was clear that the Hebrew king's request was an order Araunah could not refuse. He dropped his sword, joined the delegate, and they walked together to the Hebrews' stands, just a few hundred cubits from the Jebusites.

The wait was excruciating. Despite the crisp mountain air, Yerubaal found it hard to breathe steadily and regularly. The tension pressed his chest, as he considered what the day might bring. His mother tried to calm him with a quail soup, and, though he didn't feel like eating or drinking, he accepted it with a forced smile. The cooking seemed to be helping her calm down as much as she hoped it would calm him. He drank the soup, watching as some of his tribal warriors kept themselves busy by practicing sword fighting.

The women proceeded to prepare a meal, even though they knew many of them would not survive to eat it.

Few white clouds traveled leisurely in a blue sky. Sparrows chirped in the trees, as they always did, unaware of human struggles.

Clearly, a discussion took place between the king and Araunah in the Hebrew camp—a negotiation between two unequal sides. But none of the Jebusites had any idea what they were deliberating. If the talks failed, the tribe had no choice but to sacrifice the boy, and even that wouldn't guarantee their survival. Glancing at the high priest, Yerubaal saw him standing on the massive rock, the drinking stone. Mostly naked—except a tiny strip of cloth around his waist—he was painted with the blood of a goat he'd just slaughtered as a sacrifice. He entered a trance state, praying fervently and uttering strange words.

After a long hour, Araunah was seen walking toward his people who were anxiously waiting. On his back, he carried a small bag; on his face, he wore a huge smile of relief and triumph. Yerubaal had never seen the dour man so happy.

"We're saved, my brothers!" he called as he approached the Jebusites. "David, the great king whom God will glorify forever, does not want to destroy us!"

"So, what does he want?" called the high priest.

"He wants my threshing floor and the drinking stone. I sold it to him."

"You sold it?" The tribal people were astonished—many of them gasped, then turned to their friends, fell on each other's shoulders, and burst into spontaneous crying.

"Indeed, my dear brothers," Araunah said. "I offered to give him the threshing floor for free, but he insisted on paying me fifty silver shekels. The sons of Israel believe that the drinking stone has special significance for their religion." Araunah then looked in the direction of Yerubaal. "And you, my young friend, you can expect to have a long life."

Long life. At once, the nightmare ended. The world returned to pulse as it always had. Yerubaal managed to take a deep breath before he collapsed on the ground, overcome by uncontrolled sobbing. His parents rushed to embrace him.

"*You* did it," said his father with tears in his eyes. "You saved us."

"But I didn't do anything," Yerubaal wept.

"One day, you'll understand that it was your loyalty that saved the life of the whole tribe," his father insisted. "You could have run away, but you chose to stay and obey the will of the gods."

His mother embraced him, her hold tight as though she would never let him go.

"I don't know," she said. "Sacrificing you was the hardest thing in my life. I'm not sure I could have gone through with it. I'm so glad you're alive."

"Why does King David need the threshing floor?" The high priest turned to Araunah that evening as he sat around the campfire with Yerubaal and his family. It was after hours of celebration, and Yerubaal was ready to sleep.

"Here, the Israelites want to build a temple to their God," Araunah said. "They also plan to change the name of our city. However, they don't want to kill our people. Enough blood has been shed."

"And what name does he want to give our city?" The high priest inquired.

"Yerushaleem," Araunah answered.

Chapter 13

"Come, let me buy you lunch," McPherson said. So they stepped out of the Manhattan office building into a sunny summer day.

"I hope you don't mind walking," McPherson said.

"Not at all," Michael replied, thinking that recently he'd hardly taken the time to exercise.

The journalist led the way, and Michael followed half a step behind him. McPherson's walk was brisk and Michael was gasping. *The old man is in better shape than me.* Michael realized that he'd let McPherson's age and appearance trick him into thinking that the journalist had gotten old.

They walked in silence through the busy city. The sun beat down on Michael, making him regret his choice of long, thick pants and an unneeded jacket. His clothes began to stick to him as they continued, and he tried to mask the discomfort while attempting to keep pace with the older man. After a few turns, the city's grime faded, leaving the sidewalks a shade less gray. Fewer cars whizzed past, the bustle of people subsided, and Michael was grateful when a gentle cool breeze caressed him. McPherson continued to stride with confidence, giving Michael the impression that he knew the city like the palm of his hand. Then, the journalist abruptly turned left into a small, one-way alley.

"I like taking walks," McPherson said as he slowed down, allowing Michael to catch his breath. "While walking, I think about my projects and get my plans in order."

After a short while, McPherson opened a street door and entered a small, plain-looking store. As Michael followed him, he perceived a tiny, barely noticeable wooden signboard on top of the door, where it was hand-painted, *Helen's Deli*. Michael thought he would have never stumbled upon the place on his own.

"Stewart!" a chubby old lady behind the counter joyfully called, a giant grin breaking across her face. Her hair wrapped in a white kerchief, she had rosy cheeks and wore a light blue apron. "You should've called and given me time to prepare your favorites."

"As far as I'm concerned, Helen," McPherson said, "everything that you make is my favorite."

"And who is this handsome young man?" Helen inquired.

"That's Michael," McPherson replied. "Michael is the closest thing I will ever get to having a protégé."

"Nice to meet you." Michael nodded in Helen's direction.

"Well, what are you waiting for?" Helen said. "Stewart, you know where your table is. Why don't you take Michael over there?"

McPherson led Michael past a curtain to a small dining area with just three tables. No one else was there, so they had the place to themselves.

"How does anybody find this place?" Michael wondered.

"They don't," McPherson replied. "Helen's business is mainly in catering. The dining area is for special customers."

"I see," Michael said, perplexed as he took another glance around the room. He had no idea how McPherson managed to become a special customer everywhere he went. "And is there a menu?"

"No," McPherson said.

At Michael's baffled expression, McPherson explained, "Helen will bring us the dishes today's customers ordered. Trust me, it's gonna be good."

Helen came in, "I brought you freshly made lemonade," she said, somewhat cheerfully. "Your food will be ready in about ten minutes."

"Take your time," McPherson told her, "We're in no hurry and we've got plenty to discuss."

"We do?" Michael asked after Helen walked away.

Michael watched McPherson and was surprised to see the man's expression change. Amused and friendly while talking to Helen, he now looked utterly serious.

"Michael," McPherson opened, "taking the walk allowed me to reexamine and process this whole situation. I must tell you that it does not look good. Actually, it's quite explosive." McPherson poured himself lemonade and took a sip. "I told you that, up until today, I followed an entity that was shutting the country down every now and then, and another group that was obsessed with Isaac Newton. But now, things have changed. If Charles Bishop is behind both developments—and I'm quite certain he is—then we're facing a formidable opponent: one who is sophisticated, has a limitless amount of money, and apparently, has become a religious fanatic. Zealots scare me the most, because they're motivated by fervor, not reason, and they think they've got nothing to lose."

"So, why don't you just approach the authorities and alert them to the situation?" Michael thought that was obvious.

"And tell them what?" McPherson said. "That I have a gut feeling telling me a known American hero is dangerous? Look at his image. He's in a wheelchair after risking his life for our country, a devout Christian who donates boatloads of money to charity. He probably has local politicians as well as the media in his pockets."

Helen brought their lunch. With a satisfied smile she announced, "Gentlemen, today, we have stir-fried shrimp with vegetables and black mushrooms with rice."

She exited the room, seeming to understand that her guests needed privacy as they had important matters to discuss.

"The food here is incredible," Michael commented after several minutes of tinkling utensils and silence.

"I thought you'd like it," McPherson said, a satisfied smile working its way across his lips.

Michael took a sip of lemonade. "So, what are you suggesting?"

"Michael, this is a serious situation. I'm reluctant to ask you for a small sacrifice."

"What is it?" Michael remembered his first assignment for the journalist: McPherson had asked him to spy upon his employer. *What could it be this time?* He had an ominous feeling.

"I know how precious your family is to you ..." McPherson began.

"What on earth are you saying?"

"Look," McPherson said, "the way you are right now, you can't infiltrate the cult, not with your sweet wife and daughter and secure employment. If you approached them, they would be very suspicious about your motives. All I'm asking is that you create the *appearance* of trouble in paradise and temporarily move to another place ..."

"But, Stewart ..." Michael shook his head, trying not to gape. "Are you asking me to leave my family?"

"Just temporarily," McPherson confirmed. "Think about it as going away for an assignment."

"I'll have to think about it."

"I'm afraid time is a luxury we don't have," McPherson said firmly, meeting Michael's gaze with regret in his eyes. "Let me put it this way: World War II was probably the most horrible event in the history of humanity. It caused unimaginable pain and suffering, with millions of people killed. Let's say that we're in 1938, and *you* have the opportunity to prevent the war from ever starting. Wouldn't you do it?"

Michael took a deep breath and sighed. "It is not 1938. It's a different world now."

"How different?" McPherson argued, his fork clinking a staccato on his plate of forgotten food. "Let me draw a realistic scenario for you: Bishop and his cult are obsessed with the prophecies that fascinated Isaac Newton. They are also passionate about setting the conditions for Christ's second coming. I fear that they'll try to execute Newton's measurements and calculations and resurrect the Temple of Solomon."

"So?" Michael leaned back in his chair and scrubbed his face. Exhausted, he realized that the man he considered his mentor had come up with a plan which he couldn't refuse, even though he wished he'd never heard about it.

"Look, Michael," McPherson explained patiently, "don't you see that the only place where they could build the temple would be on the Temple Mount in Jerusalem, where it stood two thousand years ago? Otherwise, they would not be fulfilling the prophecy. At the moment, I have no idea how they plan to accomplish such a complicated task, which is why I need you to infiltrate the group."

"The Temple Mount?" Michael gazed at McPherson, trying to comprehend the meaning of his words.

"Right now, as far as I know," McPherson continued, "The place is occupied."

"Occupied?" Michael had a hard time following, sensing that the decision was already made, and once again, he was on a dangerous mission. He just wasn't sure what that mission was.

"Yes," McPherson confirmed. "There's a big rock over there. The Jews and the Christians believe it is the foundation rock which is located at the navel point of the world. On that rock, so they believe, Abraham intended to sacrifice Isaac."

"I've read about it," Michael said. "Today, there's a mosque over there."

"It is called the Dome of the Rock," McPherson said. "It's not really a mosque, but it's a beautiful structure and considered to be the third most holy place for Islam."

"So?"

"Michael," McPherson lowered his voice, leaned forward, and looked around to make sure no one was within hearing range. "If they want to rebuild the temple, we have to consider that they will blow up the Dome of the Rock ..."

"Just blow it up, huh?" A slight pressure was building at the sides of Michael's head.

"Remember," McPherson said, "religious fanatics are not motivated by reason. They are convinced that God is on their side, and *their* truth is the *only* truth."

A disturbing recollection suddenly crossed Michael's mind. "Stewart, I'm afraid there's some truth to what you're saying. On their internet site, I've seen discussions of explosives and methods of bringing down large structures."

"You see?" McPherson leaned back, threw up his arms in the air and exclaimed, "It's one more evidence that my analysis is correct. If they succeed in their plan, there will be utter outrage throughout the Muslim world. Leading religious and political leaders will call for a holy war—jihad as they call it. It will unite Muslims all over: Sunni and Shia, extremists and moderates. They will see it as their duty to liberate their sacred land, and, of course, take revenge on the perpetrators of the crime."

Michael was familiar with some Jewish practices, as his father-in-law was half Jewish. He could not help but point out in a dry tone, "As far as I know, the Jews were there before there was ever a religion called Islam."

"That's completely irrelevant!" Annoyed, McPherson waved off Michael's statement with a dismissive hand movement. "You think they care who was there first? They'll come from extremist strongholds such as Iran, the Taliban, Hamas, ISIS, Al-Qaeda, you name it, and also from more moderate places like Turkey, Pakistan, which don't forget, possesses nuclear capability, and of course from Israel's neighboring Arab countries. All these forces will have one goal in mind: to destroy the Jewish state that they will hold responsible for the action. Now, Israel probably has the strongest army in the Middle East, with a superior air force, but how long will they be able to hold?"

Warming up to the topic, McPherson's voice took on a strident note as he continued to lecture the younger man. "At some point, Israel will seek help from the United States and its NATO allies, and they will have a hard time standing by and allowing another holocaust. If the US intervenes, then how long will it be before the Russians enter the theater?

"If the US won't intervene, well, let's not forget that Israel also possesses nuclear power. Do you get the picture? And don't think for one minute that our comfortable life here in the US will continue unaffected, because it won't! We'll suffer economic hardships stemming from increased oil prices. And I haven't yet mentioned terrorism. At some point, there will be voices within the Muslim world calling for revenge against Americans and Christians, because they will figure out that an

78

American Christian group blew up their holy shrine. The result could easily be a total war, a religious confrontation between the Christian world and the Muslims. It will be what the New Testament calls Armageddon. It's quite likely that this is exactly what Bishop wants, because Armageddon, according to the Book of Revelation, will be followed by the second coming of Christ."

"But Stewart," Michael interrupted his mentor's speech, "Has there been an actual assault on the Dome of the Rock in recent history? or is this just your expert analysis of the situation?"

"There certainly were attempts," McPherson answered somberly. "The attempts were carried out by individuals as well as groups, Christians and Jews. Fortunately, the perpetrators were caught before they caused any significant damage.

"I recently came across a secretive CIA document," McPherson continued. "It states that several fundamental Christian organizations are striving to restore the ancient temple and rebuild it on the Temple Mount. The document lists the names of those groups, and Charles Bishop and his followers are not on that list. Somehow, they managed to stay undetected.

"I'd also learned about an organization of Jewish extremists that plotted to crash an airplane full of explosives on the Dome of the Rock—which they considered an abomination—but they were detained by Israeli security forces."

"Okay, Stewart, I get the picture," Michael conceded, and checked the time on his cell phone.

"Michael," McPherson said in a softer tone of voice. "It's not just your family that I'm asking you to distance yourself from."

"Who else?" Michael asked, feeling weary.

"Me," McPherson said. "From now on, we shouldn't be seen together."

"How will we communicate?"

"Someone will meet you every now and then and transfer messages between us. You should erase my name from your phone book."

Chapter 14

Tired, upset, and frustrated, Michael was not in a good mood on his way home to Brooklyn. *What will I tell Melany?*

He fell asleep on the underground train and missed his station. *Just as well,* he thought. When he awoke after the short nap, he felt better, like he managed to regenerate his strength to an extent.

Returning to his neighborhood by bus, he stopped at a corner coffee shop, and had a cup of espresso and a bagel with cream cheese.

When he arrived home, Melany sat on the sofa, reading a story to Linda, who lay curled up against her arm.

Linda looked over at Michael, a light sparkling in her green eyes at the sight of him. "Hi, Daddy," she called.

Melany paused in her storytelling to glance up at Michael with a small smile. They both had the same dimple in the same cheek as they smiled, and Michael wondered when would be the next time he'll see such bright looks on their faces.

He tried to smile at them, and Melany nodded in his direction. A knowing light brightened her eyes as she read him. She knew something had happened.

"Had a bad day?" Melany asked Michael after putting Linda to bed. She poured herself tea and sat across from him at the small kitchen table, blowing softly on the steaming mug.

He took a deep breath and sighed. "Lanie, do you know that I love you?"

"Hun," she responded, "I love you very much."

Michael's smile was gloomy. "You asked if I had a bad day. My bad day is only starting."

For a moment, she recalled when she fell in love with him. At the time, Michael had been a trainee at the television network where her father worked as a senior producer, and he'd also played in her father's amateur rock band. One evening, her father, who was fond of Michael, invited him to dinner and asked him to play and sing a song that he'd written. Melany remembered how the song, along with Michael's guitar playing and singing, had touched something deep inside her. Later, she told her father she would like to have Michael's phone number, so she could ask him out. Over the years, she asked Michael to sing that song for her on numerous occasions, and it never failed to move her.

Now she looked at him with affection and waited.

"I met with Stewart McPherson today," he said. "I already told you that I'm doing an assignment for him."

"Yes," she said, "about Newton and the cult."

"Obviously, Newton had been dead for nearly three hundred years," Michael said. "But that group I mentioned is organized, sophisticated, and well-funded, and they want to act on some of Newton's mystical ideas."

"In what way?" Melany asked with a softened voice.

"By resurrecting the Temple of Solomon," Michael replied.

"Did Newton ever aspire to do that?" she wondered.

"I don't know," Michael responded. "But he made detailed and comprehensive measurements of the temple, which he derived from the Old Testament. He believed that the temple would be rebuilt in Jerusalem, and would be even more magnificent than the original. For those who believe in biblical prophecies, it's one of the prerequisites for the return of Christ."

"Wow," she said, shaking her head. "It sounds like a volatile situation. So, their ultimate goal is the return of Jesus?"

"It appears this way," Michael said, rubbing his temples. "McPherson fears—and it's not an unfounded fear—that they plan to blow up the Muslim Dome of the Rock, on the Temple Mount in Jerusalem."

"Blow it up?" Melany's eyes widened. "Why would they want to do such a thing?"

"Because," Michael explained, "the Dome of the Rock was built right where the old temple used to stand two thousand years ago; and, if the cult's people hadn't built their temple on the exact same spot, then it wouldn't be a fulfillment of the prophecy."

Melany opened her mouth to respond, then paused to collect her thoughts. "But that's crazy!" She finally said.

"It's insane," Michael agreed, "but they are religious fanatics. When I checked their website, I saw discussions on explosives and ways to bring down large structures."

"Has McPherson tried to alert the authorities?"

"He doesn't think they'll interfere. You see, Charles Bishop, the cult's leader, is an American war hero and a billionaire. He's got a huge estate in Washington. McPherson

84

thinks that the local media and politicians won't do anything against him unless, of course, we provide hard evidence."

"Let me guess," Melany said, "Stewart wants you to infiltrate the cult and get that evidence." Her voice was just a little louder than its regular tone; still, Michael saw her furrowed eyebrows and knew she was angry.

"More or less," he said. "But, Lanie, here comes the hard part ..."

She looked into his eyes and waited, dread coiling in her gut.

"I can't do it as a happily married family man," He said somberly. "It just won't look convincing. They have to believe that I have serious marital issues and have decided to separate from my family. I would come as a lost soul looking for answers ..."

Michael stopped talking. Melany looked over his shoulder into the distance. A heavy silence hung between them.

"And you?" Melany finally spoke, "what do *you* intend to do? I guess you've already decided ..." Melany tried to smile, but the expression felt stiff on her face.

"I decided," he said. "I'm not going anywhere without your consent. Don't think for one minute that I like this plan;

but, if Stewart is right, then I have a chance and an obligation to prevent a horrible war."

She took her time pondering his words while avoiding his gaze. "How long are we talking about?"

"Not very long, I hope," he said. "I think it could be a couple of months."

"And Linda?"

"I could visit my daughter," he said. "The rest of the time—daddy is at work."

Melany got up, walked over to the window, and looked outside. She watched as the hustle and bustle of the neighborhood subsided. The sun has continued on its way; lights and TVs turned on in nearby apartment buildings, shining into the growing darkness as people prepared for their evening routines.

She turned back to him, her arms folded defensively across her chest. "So, what you're telling me is that we should break up our family because your mentor has some unfounded suspicions?"

"No, that's not what I'm telling you," he answered, his expression too calm. She could tell he was brimming with retorts, still he maintained his composure as he continued, "I'm saying that McPherson has put together an alarming theory that I can't ignore, and I'm inclined to accept. I know we're being asked to make a significant sacrifice, but how would you feel if I stayed here and did nothing, and then it turned out that he was right? And Lanie," Michael added, "the situation could easily escalate into a nuclear war. I'm sure you wouldn't want that."

She remained by the window, staring at him. He saw tears in her eyes, and his heart felt like it was breaking. For a moment, he considered giving up the whole idea and telling McPherson to find someone else.

"Lanie," he said. "I didn't mean to—"

"Okay!" she interrupted him. "Linda and I will manage. Go and do what you need to do and come back to us." She walked over to Michael, who was still sitting, and embraced him. "Oh, hun," her voice was breaking, "why did I have to marry such a righteous and moral person?" She stroked his hair. "Now, you're going to save the world, huh?"

"Only if you let me," he whispered. He pressed his ear to her belly and heard her heart beating.

Chapter 15

For the event of things predicted many ages before, will then be a convincing argument that the world is governed by providence. For as the few and obscure Prophecies concerning Christ's first coming were for setting up the Christian religion, which all nations have since corrupted; so the many and clear Prophecies concerning the things to be done at Christ's second coming, are not only for predicting but also for effecting a recovery and re-establishment of the long-lost truth, and setting up a kingdom wherein dwells righteousness.

- **Issac Newton, Observations upon the Prophecies of Daniel and the Apocalypse of St. John.**

The school year was over, and it was time for the summer vacation. It would be a long time before Michael would have to teach again since he'd arranged to take a sabbatical over the next academic year.

He moved to a low-budget, extended-stay hotel, but remained in Brooklyn so that he could be close to his home and family. He continued to log onto the group's website and participate in discussions.

On the *His Time* site, *Saint Miriam* continued to remind people that the momentous day was coming soon, but she didn't indicate when that might be.

Michael spent much of his time reading Newton's books and related Christian prophecies. At night, he went to bars, drank beer by himself, and returned to the hotel at late hours. He stopped shaving and just trimmed his beard occasionally with scissors. From time to time, he hung around a nearby park where he played the blues on his guitar. He didn't beg for money but didn't object when, occasionally, people threw coins into his guitar case. Strangely, the few coins he made by playing the guitar gave him a greater sense of accomplishment than the fat check he received from the university. *In my heart, I always remained a musician,* he realized.

He visited a church several times, sat in the back, and wondered why anybody would care to follow him. Within a short time, Michael was no longer sure whether he played a lost soul or if he had become one.

He wondered how long he could sustain this new lifestyle, recognizing that a part of it actually appealed to him. He was free and didn't have to report to anyone. He could get up whenever he wanted and hang out wherever he felt like. He could eat junk food and didn't even have to tie his shoes. When had he ever had such freedom? He was always a goal-oriented person who never stopped calculating his moves. Perhaps, in some strange way, he'd stumbled upon a real vacation?

One night, he went to a bar not far from the hotel. He'd been there before and liked the place more than other bars in the area because it was relatively quiet—the hard-rock and soft-metal music were played at a reasonable level, allowing Michael to tune it out if he wished.

He ordered a pint of beer and took his time, drinking at the counter. Looking around, he sensed the atmosphere of misery that hung in the air like a dense fog. Mostly lone individuals filtered in and out to sit alone in the booths that lined the walls, leaving the several tall, circular tables between the bar and booths deserted. Some of the patrons tried to look happy and even attempted to start conversations with the bartender or the waitress, but in the end, they were left alone, unable to escape their loneliness.

After about an hour of gnawing on pretzels and observing the day's news on the bar's TV, he noticed a good-looking, blonde woman sitting on the other end of the bar. She spoke loudly to the bartender, occasionally laughing for what seemed like no reason.

Michael noticed a contradiction between the lady's sleazy behavior and her modest appearance. She wore an elegant black dress—that he thought was a type of outfit his female friends would wear when they went out—and had makeup that highlighted her attractive features, rather than obscuring them with loud colors or glitter.

From his best estimate, the woman was somewhere in her mid-twenties. She noticed him looking in her direction and smiled at him, a dark twinkle in her eye. Michael didn't bother smiling back.

Why would such a lady come to a place like this and get drunk? He wondered. *Perhaps she broke up with her boyfriend? Or maybe she's just having a bad day?*

She could have been a prostitute, but Michael didn't think she was. He couldn't help but ponder about her; what else was there to focus on in that dark, gloomy bar?

Checking the time on his cell phone, Michael realized it was quite late. He paid the bartender and turned to go, but the young lady stood in his path and blocked his way.

"Already leaving?" she asked, giving him a playful smile. "Such a handsome man shouldn't spend the night alone."

"I'm sorry," he said politely, trying not to be rude. "I really have to go now."

"Well, at least let me give you my phone number," she said, "just in case, you know, you might get lonely." She searched in her handbag. "By the way," she said while pulling out a small notebook and a pen, "my name is Rachel."

Michael nodded to signal that he heard her but didn't bother introducing himself.

She jotted something on the notebook with her pen, ripped out the page, and handed him the note. "There you go!" she chirped. "You can call me anytime!"

Michael took the note. "See you," he muttered and headed for the door. *I'm not looking for an affair*, he reminded himself, *I'm a married man*. When the door closed behind him, he peeked at the note as he approached a trash can.

The message stunned him, made him stop in his tracks, turn, and step back into the bar. It wasn't a telephone number that she'd handed him, but a simple mathematical equation: $360 \times 7 = 2520$.

She smiled when Michael approached her. "I see that you changed your mind."

"I did," he grumbled.

"Good decision!" she exclaimed and grabbed his arm as he turned to leave again. From the corner of his eye, Michael saw the bartender smiling and signaling him with a thumbs-up.

Michael waved down a taxi, even though he was within walking distance of the hotel. He opened the door for his companion and sat next to her, wondering who sent her. During the short drive, the lady sat quietly without crowding him or trying to embrace him as he feared she might. They arrived at the hotel, where Michael helped her out of the car. Once again, the woman behaved as though drunk, leaning on him in a clumsy manner.

He helped her walk to the elevator and guided her to his hotel apartment. Upon entering the room, the woman's demeanor once again changed. She grabbed her hair and removed what was apparently a wig. Now exposed from beneath the wig, her short, brunette hair glimmered in the room's soft glow, complementing the splash of freckles across her tan face and her lively, playful green eyes. Her tight black dress and needle-point heels accentuated the soft curves of her slim, athletic body."

"Hi, Michael," she said in a relaxed voice and extended her hand. "Let me introduce myself again. My name is Rachel, and I work for Stewart McPherson."

"Is that your real name?" he asked suspiciously and shook her hand.

"Yes," she confirmed. "I'll sleep on the sofa."

"The sofa would be fine for you," he agreed. "It has a better mattress than the bed."

"I've slept in worse places," she said and threw her handbag on the sofa.

"Was all that show necessary?" He asked.

"Yes," she answered. "I had to introduce myself, and you needed to establish your new status as a man estranged from his wife."

"Does Stewart think that anybody is watching me?"

"It's a distinct possibility. It's safe to assume that they have access to every camera in town, be it a street camera or a device installed in a store. So, they don't need to follow you physically."

94

"Any news from Stewart?" Michael asked.

"Not right now," Rachel replied. "He wants you to be extra careful and communicate through me. I'll be around."

Michael nodded. *Here I am,* he reflected, *in a hotel room with an attractive woman who is not my wife.* He hoped the night would be uneventful.

Chapter 16

On a warm summer afternoon, Michael stepped out to get
some necessities at a nearby store. Returning with a bag full of
groceries and entering his hotel suite, a strange feeling
overcame him. Glancing all over, he saw that nothing was
missing or appeared different than when he left, but his
instincts prickled. Was there another presence in the room?
Setting down the groceries, he quickly passed through the
living room, bedroom, and kitchenette. Everything seemed to
be in order. It wasn't a robbery, he noted with relief. Thieves
left messes behind as they rushed, looking for valuables.

Then he noticed that the lid of his laptop computer, located
on a small table near his bed, was open, and Michael didn't
remember if he'd left it that way. He usually closed the lid
when he was away, to prevent the accumulation of dust, but
perhaps he'd run off in a hurry and hadn't remembered to
close it.

While advancing toward the computer, he couldn't see if there was anything on the screen, since the laptop faced away from him.

He walked over, and once his computer screen was within sight, noticed the camera's light was on, suggesting it was being used.

By whom?

Suspiciously, he approached the computer. Someone was on the screen, watching. Michael's heartbeat quickened. *What's going on?* It was like stumbling upon a burglar.

When he was finally in front of the screen, he discovered his intruder was a woman. She looked curiously at him, observed his movements, and didn't try to hide her presence.

"Who are you?" he asked, trying to maintain his composure, though his skin tingled all over.

"Hi, Michael," she said in a warm voice.

"Who the hell are you?" he demanded, "and how did you break into my secured computer?"

"I'm Mary," she said pleasantly.

"Mary? Is that supposed to mean anything to me?"

"Of course, Michael." She smiled at him.

Michael was angry about the invasion of his privacy — or he knew he was supposed to feel angry. He couldn't help but notice that his invader was a strikingly beautiful woman.

Her complexion was dark, her long hair darker, curling around a shoulder and accentuating her alluring, clear blue eyes. She wasn't young; Michael thought she was in her forties. Her smile was mysterious and knowing, welcoming Michael in on a secret.

"Mary," he said. "What is this all about?"

"We've communicated before," she said. "You've asked a question, and I'm here to provide an answer."

"I don't know you," Michael said. *Could she be a representative of the cult?*

"You do know me," she said patiently. "We met at the forum. You called yourself *Angel Mikhael*, while I posed as *Saint Miriam*."

Michael sensed how the blood rushed into his face. So, now the cult has contacted him directly. They knew who he was, and they had the means to reach him.

"I don't remember leaving my computer on," he muttered.

"You didn't," she confirmed. "We know a thing or two about technology; but, that's really not the issue here, so let's not waste time. You asked a valuable question on our forum.

Your question was whether there's a connection between the measurements of Solomon's temple and our solar system, as Isaac Newton suggested."

"That's true," Michael said. "So, what's your answer?"

"You will get your answer in a few minutes," she somberly said. "Now, we know that you've been lurking on our site for some time. We know that you recently separated from your wife. We also know that you've been drinking and having an affair with someone you picked up in a bar. Am I right so far?"

"Sounds about right," Michael confirmed.

"Michael," she said, and looked directly into his eyes. "We assess that you are a true seeker, but drinking and having casual sex isn't the solution for your soul. If you are prepared to tread the path, then you have to get serious, and you must commit to fighting for the truth."

Her gaze conveyed utter solemnity as she maintained deep and prolonged eye contact, and yet, Michael sensed a halo of seduction surrounding her.

"I'm still waiting for an answer to my question," Michael said.

"I can introduce you to someone who will answer your question and other questions, including questions you haven't thought of yet," she said. "If you're done with playing games, and you know with every fiber of your being that it's time to move on, then I'm here to arrange it."

"I'm ready," Michael sat in front of her, hoping he appeared trustworthy.

"Fine," she said. "Let me tell you that you're about to meet our leader, the *Ark Bishop*. He specifically requested to talk to you, which is a great honor. I hope you understand that you are at a turning point in your life. The only thing we ask of you is total sincerity and commitment."

"I'd be honored to speak with him," Michael said.

Chapter 17

Melany

I started writing notes to myself. It's not really a diary, I think. I never had a diary and never felt the need to write one. But now that Michael is away, I sometimes need to express my thoughts. I guess one could call it a diary. So, dear diary:

Maybe our lives aren't as perfect as I thought. There are times when it feels like Michael and I live next to each other, but not *with* one another. I noticed that, over time, we started to take each other for granted. Perhaps it's unavoidable and a natural process that occurs in every marriage. I've no prior experience as I've never been married before.

I was in other relationships before I met Michael, but it never felt so right as with him. I felt that way ever since the day my dad invited him to our house and he sang the song that he wrote. There was something real about him, honest, not fake like some other guys I knew.

With time, I began to realize that Michael is a little damaged. It's not like it sounds. I'm not saying it as a negative thing. On the contrary, it's a reason to love him even more. Still, at times I think that Michael never overcame growing up as an adopted child, despite having a great adoptive family who truly loved him. I think that Michael was deeply disturbed when he found that his biological father had sexually abused his birth mother, drugged, and essentially raped her. So, I think that deep inside, Michael, who is such a sensitive soul, is afraid that he could turn out to be a bit like his father.

I'm not sure if this whole story about Newton and the cult is not just an excuse to go away and search for answers. Our daughter Linda is already five years old. I think by now we should have had another child, but Michael says that we have to wait until we have a house of our own and that the planet is already overpopulated, and other such excuses.

There's a new guy at work, Henry. We have a good connection and good conversations. I was honest with him and told him that I love my husband, who is away. Henry knows that Michael joined a crazy cult that wants to bring on a world war so that Jesus will return.

I know I should have been more secretive.

102

Henry is divorced. He frequently asks me out, and we go to expensive restaurants and movies. He has a lot of money, a fancy house, and he drives a Ferrari. At times it seems that he wants more from me than my friendship. I think that even though he knows I'm married, he wants to get in my pants, but he won't say it. I know without any doubt that he doesn't have a chance. Maybe I'm at fault here, for being a bit of a flirt, enjoying the attention of another man and making him think that anything could develop beyond friendship. But now that Michael is gone, I'm lonelier than usual, and, at my age, the attention is flattering.

Chapter 18

"Newton regarded the universe as a cryptogram set by the Almighty, just as himself wrapped the discovery of the calculus in a cryptogram... He looked on the whole universe and all that is in it as a riddle, as a secret which could be read by applying pure thought to certain evidence, certain mystic clues which God had laid about the world to allow a sort of philosopher's treasure hunt..."

- ***John Maynard Keynes**[2]*

Mary vanished from the screen, and her presence was replaced by a 3D animated clip of the solar system in motion. Sitting in front of the computer in his apartment, Michael waited as the video faded into an image of the Temple of Solomon. Strangely, though, Michael had the impression that the temple being displayed differed from other models he'd seen before. Those were either small replicas built according

---

[2] *The World of Mathematics* (2000 ed.). Dover. p. 277.

to specifications found in the Bible or 3D computerized models.

The temple now shown on his screen looked like a film of an actual structure. It was standing in a large meadow where the trees in the background gently swayed in the wind.

After about a minute, the picture faded, and Michael found himself facing a man who smiled as he examined him.

"Praise be to God," he said, "I'm Charles Bishop. I'm glad to meet you finally."

"It's an honor," Michael replied while examining the cult's leader. Bishop was a good-looking man who seemed to be in his fifties; he had long, thick gray hair, a matching beard, and large green eyes. His gaze was inquisitive; still, it conveyed kindness and empathy. Dressed in informal white clothes, he sat upright in his wheelchair.

"I was told," Bishop said, "that you are a sincere spiritual seeker."

"I never defined it that way," Michael responded, "but I've always searched for the truth."

"I know that you teach journalism at a respected university," Bishop said.

"True," Michael said, scouring his brain for the right thing to say, "though recently, I've been questioning every aspect of my life."

"Then you came to the right place." Bishop's smile appeared genuine and welcoming.

"I have questions," Michael said.

"Of course, we'll get to your questions in a minute," Bishop said patiently. "Michael, I have to be honest with you. Before I asked for this meeting, I requested a background check on you. I understand that you were adopted and that, as a grown man, you searched and found your biological mother."

"It's true," Michael said. He knew Bishop's resources were practically limitless. If Bishop instructed his people to conduct a background check on him, what else did they find?

Michael liked Bishop's deep and pleasant voice. Bishop's words had the ring of truth, like he knew in his very soul that every word he spoke was indisputable.

Just ten minutes after they'd met, and Michael thought he could already understand how people would follow this charismatic man wherever he led them.

Talking about his adoption circumstances usually made Michael uncomfortable, but not that time. When Bishop brought up his background, his voice carried utmost care and compassion, which made Michael feel as if he were talking to a spiritual father, or perhaps, to the biological father he wished he could have had.

"I read some of your articles," Bishop said, hauling Michael from his thoughts.

Michael blinked, his brows shooting up.

"I find that you present your theses and opinions clearly and coherently."

"Thank you," Michael responded. "Coming from you, that means a lot to me."

"Fine, Michael," Bishop said, leaning back comfortably in his wheelchair and meeting Michael's gaze. "Please ask your questions, and I'll answer them as best as I can."

Michael focused. For a split second, those questions didn't seem all that important. "I have difficulty," he finally said, "with some of the concepts attributed to Newton. For example, the idea that there's a correlation between the measurements of the temple and those of the universe, or at least our solar system."

Bishop nodded. "I appreciate your candor and skepticism. I intend to lead my people to great achievements, but I want them to act from deep conviction and not through blind faith." Bishop took a sip from a glass of water, and then gently set his glass down on a desk that Michael couldn't see. "In my opinion, Isaac Newton was the greatest scientist of all time. By *scientist*, I mean what we consider his scientific discoveries as well as his work in the field of theology. I don't separate the two as the scientific community does."

Bishop paused and looked at Michael as if to see that he got the point and agreed. When Michael nodded, he continued, "You probably know that Newton spent a great deal of time figuring the exact measurements of Solomon's Temple. He drew most of the information from the Old Testament, but he had to adjust the data to the measuring units of his time. So, he converted the Hebrew cubits into feet and inches. Then, he inserted a whole chapter about the temple's configuration with precise measurements in his book *The Chronology of Ancient Kingdoms*."

"Yes, but how do those measurements relate to the solar system?" Michael insisted.

"Patience, young man," Bishop said, "You see, in the middle of a book that otherwise deals exclusively with history and time, Newton inserted an entire chapter that is a detailed description of the Temple of Solomon. To me, it's a clear indication of his understanding that time and space are one

108

and the same. In that sense, he preceded Albert Einstein, no doubt, another incredible genius. And Einstein used some of Newton's breakthrough ideas, like differential calculus, to express his theory of general relativity."

Mary entered the left corner of the screen and approached Bishop to whisper in his ear. Bishop nodded and turned back to face Michael. "I have to stop now to attend to another important matter. Let's continue tomorrow at the same time." He seemed to be checking his calendar. "Tomorrow at 6:00 PM?"

"I'll be here," Michael promised.

Chapter 19

Jerusalem 586 BC

Little Abigail was scared. She wanted so much for things to return to the way they were before the siege. But after more than two years of being surrounded, she had a hard time remembering what it was like.

She tried not to think about the war, about what could happen to her, to her parents and little brother, but the worry was everywhere. She saw it in peoples' eyes, in their subdued behavior, silence, and fear. The grown-ups who had always smiled at her were now avoiding her or responding with agitation when she asked anything.

She didn't have to look far. Just strolling along the city wall as she used to wasn't the same. The Jewish soldiers prepared to defend their city, sharpening their swords, preparing arrows, practicing one-on-one combat, and she was getting in their way. If she dared gaze beyond the fortified walls, she saw the enormous Babylonian army. Their camps stretched over great distances—tents covering the rocky landscape, soldiers dressed in shiny armor, colorful horses, elegant chariots, and massive war machines.

They looked so frightening as they prepared for an assault that would destroy everything that she held dear. At times the fear was so gripping, it threatened to paralyze her and made breathing difficult.

Several times, Abigail climbed to the upper section of the wall, where firing slits were carved into the rough gray bricks. Watching through an embrasure, she imagined how she would shoot flaming arrows at the Babylonians and scare them away.

Although Abigail was merely nine years old, she understood how grave the situation was. For months, she'd listened to grown-ups' arguments—her parents, teachers, parents of her friends, and community leaders. One night, she eavesdropped on her parents, who sat by the fireplace in their brick home, and thought she was sleeping.

"I wish King Zedekiah had just paid his taxes to Babylon," her mother said, her voice trembling. "Then, this war could have been avoided. Our kingdom is too small and weak to stand against the powerful Babylonian Empire."

"We have God on our side, Devorah," Abigail's father replied. "He will not allow the fall of Jerusalem and his holy temple built by King Solomon."

"But I heard the prophet Jeremiah," Devora said. "You heard him too, Joshua. He says the Babylonians will completely demolish Jerusalem."

"Jeremiah claims to speak in the name of God," Abigail's father tried to sound confident. "Well, I'm not sure he's not just a crazy old man."

"Crazy or not; unfortunately, he could be right." Devorah said, "I also heard that the Babylonian King Nebuchadnezzar is extremely cruel."

"Let me remind you," Joshua said, "that the Assyrians, who conquered and destroyed the kingdom of Israel and most of the kingdom of Judea, failed to conquer Jerusalem. I also know that King Zedekiah sent messengers to ask for aid from Egypt."

"I know that," Devorah said. "But Jeremiah warns that God is displeased with King Zedekiah," Devorah's voice was about to crack, "which is why the Babylonians will prevail where the Assyrians failed."

112

"We'll fight them," Joshua promised. "And don't forget how well our city is fortified."

"I'm so scared for our children," Devora said.

And then Abigail heard her mother weep.

The final battle raged for several days. Abigail saw the massive dike that the Babylonians built. She saw their war machines hammering the fortified walls, and she prayed for a miracle. She was hungry and thirsty, as were all the inhabitants of Jerusalem. The defending soldiers were exhausted, while the Babylonians, despite suffering heavy casualties, kept coming with fresh reinforcements.

Then came the inevitable. King Nebuchadnezzar's soldiers broke through Jerusalem's walls and conquered the city. Little Abigail heard that King Zedekiah escaped, but the Babylonians captured and blinded him. Jerusalem's survivors, mostly women and children, were rounded up and kept behind a fence. They were told to prepare for the long march to exile in Babylon, where they were destined to be slaves for the rest of their lives.

From where she was jailed, Abigail, tightly clinging to her mother, watched the Babylonians as they plundered, demolished, and razed the city to the ground, just as the prophet Jeremiah warned. Abigail knew she would never see her father again. She wept when she saw the Temple of Solomon being destroyed and set on fire.

Chapter 20

And he (King Solomon) made a molten sea, ten cubits from the one brim to the other: it was round all about, and his height was five cubits: and a line of thirty cubits did compass it round about.

25 It stood upon twelve oxen, three looking toward the north, and three looking toward the west, and three looking toward the south, and three looking toward the east: and the sea was set above upon them, and all their hinder parts were inward.

26 And it was a hand breadth thick, and the brim thereof was wrought like the brim of a cup, with flowers of lilies: it contained two thousand baths.

- ***Old Testament – 1 Kings 7:23***

Exactly at 6:00 PM, Michael's computer woke up from sleep mode, the camera turned on, seemingly by itself, and Mary appeared on the screen.

"Hello, Michael," she had a slight smile on her face.

"Hi, Mary," he responded, and once again, he was struck by her unusual, alluring beauty. *She's probably from South America*, he thought.

"I will now transfer you to the *Ark Bishop*," she said as she gazed at him with her clear blue eyes.

"Fine." His focus sharpened as adrenaline pounded into his blood.

Mary disappeared, and the view on the screen turned into the 3D animated graphic demonstrating the solar system in motion. It dissolved into the video of the temple standing in a meadow, where tree branches swayed in the background, and after a few seconds, the image dissolved again, and once more, Michael faced Charles Bishop.

"Praise be to God," Bishop smiled at him with affection. "We will now continue where we left off."

"That would be great," Michael said.

"Clearly," Bishop said after taking a sip of water, "when Newton said there's a correlation between the temple and the solar system, he didn't necessarily mean that they have the same shape."

"I assumed so," Michael said.

"Like other learned scholars of his time," Bishop continued, "Newton invested significant effort in deciphering ancient scriptures. He was convinced that over the years, many belief systems degenerated into idolatry, including segments of Christianity. Along with that, he believed that

116

ancient scriptures contained the secrets of the universe, together with knowledge of astronomy and physics, in an encoded form. He also asserted that ancient theology didn't distinguish between religion and science.

"Therefore, it was only natural for him to extract information from old biblical and Talmudic descriptions of the temple and the tabernacle."

"Did he succeed?" Michael asked.

"Great question." Bishop smiled. "You know, most people think that by discovering gravity, Newton merely explained why an apple falls from the tree to the ground. In fact, he used the gravitational force to explain rules within our solar system. What keeps planets in orbit, and our moon and comets in their trajectories is the same force, gravity, that made the apple fall down. Today, most scholars tend to agree that Newton's story about the apple that triggered him to ponder gravity is not true. I go along with those scholars and believe that Newton created that fable because he wanted to hide the real source of his discovery."

"In the configuration of the temple?" Michael asked, eyes widening with amazement.

"That's right, young man," Bishop confirmed. "You see, Newton believed that the temple was designed with divine intervention. As such, its dimensions and proportions represented solutions to mathematical problems, such as the calculations for the constant pi squared[3], which obviously is the same on earth and elsewhere in the solar system."

"Fascinating," Michael said.

"Now, Michael, this is important to understand, which is why your question is so valuable. If we examine the description of Solomon's Temple, found in the Bible, we come across a detailed portrayal of an unusual structure called *The Molten Sea*, which stood in the inner court of the temple. It was a gigantic round basin, made of brass, used as a water reservoir for the ceremonial cleansing of the priests—the kohanim. According to the Bible, it contained enough water for two thousand baths."

Mesmerized, Michael hung onto every word. He felt that Bishop bestowed him with exceptional knowledge and shared secrets that most people are unaware of.

"The Basin, the Bible tells us," Bishop continued, "was placed on the backs of twelve statues of oxen, also made out of brass or bronze." Bishop looked solemnly at Michael

---

[3] "π," Pi, also called Archimedes constant, generally abbreviated to 3.14.

through the computer's camera. "Now, Michael, I have a riddle for you."

Michael nodded, somewhat apprehensively.

"There are twelve statues of oxen holding the basin," Bishop said. "All of them are facing away from the center of the basin. Three are facing east, three are facing west, three face north, and three face south. The basin is extremely heavy. These are statues of oxen, of course, not living animals, but I look at it as an incredible metaphor, and I believe so did Sir Isaac Newton. The question is: what kept the oxen in place while carrying the heavy weight? What prevented them from running away? ..."

Michael took his time pondering the riddle. He felt that he was given an important test, an assessment, although Bishop didn't express it as such.

"Following the metaphor," Michael said slowly, "I believe the basin represents the sun," Michael looked at Bishop, hoping for a sign of approval.

"Go on," Bishop encouraged him. Bishop's eyes narrowed a bit as he observed every little movement that Michael made.

"The oxen represent the planets," Michael continued. He saw Bishop nodding.

"Gravity!" Michael whispered. "That's what keeps the planets in their trajectories, and that's what kept the oxen from running away." He didn't know why his eyes were moist. Michael felt as if he'd just passed an initiation ritual.

Bishop beamed with delight. "Michael, your original question was why Newton saw a connection between the Temple of Solomon and the solar system, and you've just answered it yourself." Bishop took another slow, deliberate sip from his glass of water. "I could tell you more about Newton and my mission; however, I prefer to do it in person."

A tingle ran up and down Michael's spine.

"I'd like you to visit my estate. I don't extend such invitations lightly. Are you interested?" Bishop asked quietly, raising his eyebrows ever so slightly.

"Definitely!"

"I only invite selected people whom I feel I can trust, and I have specific roles for them in my plan."

"Do you have a role for me?"

"Absolutely, Michael. I told you that I read several of your articles. I find you eloquent and logical. You present your arguments in a clear, intelligent, and convincing way. I like how you keep your explanations simple, and you don't slip into artificial academic jargon that is arrogant and

120

cumbersome, and doesn't get the point across; thus, I have chosen you to be our spokesman. I place great importance on this position, especially since my physical condition prevents me from being with my people and representing them every step of the way. Lately, I've received distinct signals that the time for action is near. I'd be delighted to have you on board."

"I'm flattered," Michael said, shyly. He slightly bowed his head toward Bishop, whose words filled him with excited anticipation. "I hope I won't let you down."

"Now," Bishop said with a gracious smile, "I will leave you with Mary, so she'll make the arrangements for your arrival. Praise be to God, the Father of our Lord Jesus Christ."

"Praise be," Michael echoed, perplexed, as he wasn't sure what was the proper way to answer Bishop's blessing. For a moment, he felt guilty about the deception and not being honest with the charming man confined to a wheelchair.

Bishop grabbed both wheels of his wheelchair and rolled backward until he vanished from the camera's view. The display on Michael's screen reverted to the 3D animation of the solar system.

While waiting, Michael reflected on his meeting with the cult's charismatic leader. Bishop radiated empathy, compassion, even fatherhood. He didn't look like someone who strived to bring on a world war, an apocalypse, Armageddon. Michael wondered whether his perception of Bishop was influenced and skewed by the fact that he still sought a spiritual father to replace the biological father he never had.

Michael immediately reminded himself of the great danger that Bishop posed, at least according to Stewart McPherson.

After several minutes, the picture dissolved again into the temple, then switched to Mary's face.

"Hello, Michael," she said.

"Hello, Mary," Michael replied.

"My name, by the way, is Mary Bishop. I'm his wife."

"Well then," he said, heat creeping up his face, "hello, Mrs. Bishop."

"Feel free to call me Mary. Now, to the task at hand: we need to get you over here, right?"

"Yes," he nodded.

"Are you familiar with the State of Washington?" she asked.

"Not at all," he said. "I've only been there twice, and that was—"

"Never mind," she interrupted, her forehead crinkling momentarily as she thought fast. "You should fly to Seattle, and then take a bus to Olympia. We'll reimburse you for the travel expenses. In Olympia, get a room at the St. George Hotel. That's all you need to do. The hotel's staff will inform us of your arrival, and we'll send someone to pick you up within a day or two. Any questions?"

Hmm, he thought, *this is one no-nonsense woman.* "What's the weather like?"

"At this time of year, it's quite dry and warm; but, it's always a good idea to carry a raincoat with you. It could get wet here in the forest."

"Thank you, Mary."

"We'll see you soon."

Chapter 21

After his conversation with Charles Bishop and Mary, Michael prepared himself a cup of tea in the kitchenette of his hotel apartment. *Quite a development*, he reflected. *I'll have to leave my comfort zone where I've just been lurking, and I won't be close to Melany and Linda anymore.* He wished he could have hugged his wife and daughter right there and then.

Since Bishop's people could access his computer from anywhere, Michael closed his laptop's lid and pulled the plug. He knew that with the battery still in place, a sophisticated hacker could gain some control over his laptop, but at least operating the camera was not possible.

He called Rachel, his contact with Stewart McPherson.

"Hi, honey," she cheerfully answered. "Did you miss me?"

"I sure did," he said. "Could you come to my place? I could really use a woman's company."

"Not just any woman, I hope," she said.

"Of course not," he said. "I miss *you*."

"I could be there around nine o'clock this evening. Is that okay?

"That would be great."

Shortly after 9:00 PM, Michael heard a knock on the door. When he opened it, he saw Rachel, wearing the blond wig, standing on high heels, and cradling a bottle of wine. She leaned forward, hugged him with her free arm, and kissed him passionately on his lips as she kicked the door shut behind her.

As soon as the door closed, she released him. She looked for the light switch and flipped it off. The room darkened except for a little light coming from the kitchen.

"Well," she said, "some jobs are more fun than others."

She removed the wig and shook out her hair.

Michael turned off his phone and signaled Rachel to do the same. He assumed that if Bishop's people could use the computer's camera to spy on him, they could do the same with cell phones. As with the computer, Michael knew that he was not completely protected without removing the batteries, but he believed he made it harder for anyone to observe him.

"You're quite an actress," Michael told Rachel after she turned off her phone.

"I took acting in college, in addition to history and political science," she explained. "After school, though, I decided to be a private investigator, and now my acting skills are being put to the test."

"You know they saw me picking up a blonde at a bar?"

"I thought they would follow you, Michael. These are some serious people. They don't play around."

Michael nodded as he considered the risk that he was taking in his involvement with those "serious people."

"So, what did you want to see me about?" Rachel asked.

"I'm going to Bishop's land," he said.

"Wow, now, that's a development." She contemplated his announcement for a moment while tapping a finger to her chin. "So, does that mean that they're preparing for action?"

"Possibly. I have to fly to Seattle, and from there I'll go to Olympia by bus. They'll pick me up from a hotel called *The St. George.*"

"Do you know if they have a specific role for you?" Rachel asked.

"I do. I think that if they didn't have a role for me, they wouldn't invite me. Anyway, I'm going to be their spokesman when Charles isn't around. You know he's confined to a wheelchair."

126

"Michael," she looked at him with appreciation, "you must have left quite an impression on him."

"I think I did, but—" something bothered him.

"But what?"

"I'm deceiving them, Rach."

"Michael, you must not forget who we're dealing with, and the catastrophe they intend to create."

Michael noticed how her eyes became hard and cold as stones in winter, all amusement gone from her tanned golden face.

"Such fanatics," she continued, "will do anything to accomplish their crazy objectives."

"You're right," he said, amazed at the change in her, and how serious she became. "Incidentally, do you know how I will communicate with Stewart once I'm in Washington?"

"I'll follow you to Olympia. I heard it's beautiful up there."

"But, don't you have other projects?" he wondered.

"Most of my work is in doing research online, so I can do that anywhere. Of course, Stewart is paying for my expenses, and I don't think he'll stop at this moment."

"He won't," Michael said.

"Not when you're getting close to your target. I believe you'll need me."

"Did you talk to him recently?" Michael asked.

"Yep, we talk regularly. He asked me to tell you to get him recordings of Bishop."

"Recordings of Bishop?" Michael echoed, wondering how he would pull that off. "I... hope I can do it. Sounds a bit risky."

"Here," she said and handed him a tiny electronic device. "Although it's small, it's a powerful digital recorder. It can pick up a signal from about thirty feet away. You can record up to a hundred hours on it. But you're right, you should use extreme caution. If you suspect that they're onto you, stop immediately."

"Do you know what Stewart needs this recording for?" Michael asked.

"Something technological that Irene is working on. You know, she's quite a computer genius."

"And they're quite a team."

"Actually, they're amazing," Rachel said, her face glowing with admiration. "I hope I'll be so loving with my partner when I'm at their age."

"I'm curious," Michael said. "How does a young lady choose to become a private investigator?"

128

"My mother was a history teacher, and my family expected me to follow in her footsteps. I couldn't stand that they all knew what was best for me, and teaching seemed awfully boring; so, I rebelled and went for something that looked way more challenging."

"And how did they accept it?" He wondered.

"Not so well at first, but I think they learned to respect my choice. Besides, I'm not the only black sheep in our family."

Michael checked his wristwatch. "Let's order a pizza and then go to sleep," he suggested.

"I'd rather have Chinese food," Rachel said, smirking.

"Chinese it is," he agreed.

"Incidentally," she said, "which sofa do you want me to sleep on tonight?" She laughed, as clearly—his hotel apartment only had one sofa.

"You can sleep in the bed tonight," Michael said.

"Michael?" She examined him; eyebrows raised in surprise.

"*I* will sleep on the sofa," he clarified, feeling embarrassed.

She sighed. "You sure had me fooled."

"Sorry," he said, "I didn't mean to mislead you. If I weren't married …"

"That's okay," she said. "Don't worry about it."

Michael took a deep breath. *I should be strong,* he told himself, wondering what further challenges his assignment has in store for him.

Chapter 22

"Daddy!" Linda, who opened the door, threw herself in his arms. "Did you come back to live with us, Daddy?"

"Not today, sweetie, but pretty soon."

"Promise? Cross your heart and hope to die," she demanded, pulling out of the hug and crossing her tiny arms.

Michael laughed. "Where did you learn this one, sweetie? Of course, I promise."

"Mommy! Daddy is here!" Linda ran to the kitchen.

Melany came towards him. She smiled, but it didn't quite reach her eyes. Michael opened his arms to her, and after a pause, Melany stepped into them and embraced him. Linda, running up from the kitchen, pounced on them, determined not to be left out of the family hug.

"Linda, sweetie," Michael said, "how about you go and play in your room for a while? Mommy and Daddy need to talk."

"Can I watch TV?"

"You sure can."

Michael and his wife went to his small, deserted, home office and shut the door behind them.

"So?" Melany asked, "are you still chasing the bad guys? Or are they chasing after you?"

The room's dim light did little to lift the shadows crowding around them, obscuring parts of Melany's stony face.

"Lanie," he said, "you know I didn't ask for this job. Please be patient just a little bit longer."

"What did you want to talk about?" she asked dryly.

Michael observed how her shoulders slumped as if she was exhausted. His heart went out to her.

"How are you holding up?" He asked gently, "Are your parents helping with Linda?"

"They do. Dad wants an exclusive interview with you for his network when it's all done."

"That would be okay with me," Michael said.

"I got mad at him for even thinking about it and told him to forget it."

"Your father's a good man."

"I have a feeling," Melany cut in, giving him a dull stare, "that you came to tell me something."

"True," he said. "I'm going to Washington—the state, not D.C., and there's a chance that, from there, I'll go to Jerusalem. I won't be able to visit you for the next month or so."

"Will you be able to call us?" Her eyebrows rose, but her lips tightened.

"I'll try. They know that I have a daughter, so they'd understand if I'd want to talk to her."

"Will you be in danger?"

"I don't think so. I may be their spokesman."

"Congratulations on your new job." Her smile was bitter.

"Are you leaving, Daddy?" Linda asked.

"I have to go, sweetie. Come, give me a hug."

She clicked off the TV, climbed over the back of the couch, and leapt into his awaiting arms.

"Why did you grow your beard, Daddy?"

"Do you like it?"

"Hmm," she crinkled her nose, "not so much."

"And why do you wear a pink shirt, sweetie?"

"Because Mommy bought it for me."

"I tell you what, when I come back, I'll shave the beard."

"Promise?"

"Promise."

He left the house and continued on his way, but that wasn't the farewell he was hoping for. Melany. He couldn't help but sense a growing distance between them. An intimacy that wasn't there. Did he let her down? Was the separation too hard on her?

Chapter 23

From Seattle, Michael took a bus to Olympia, the capital of Washington. He used the flight and the bus ride to reflect on the direction recent developments had taken him. Michael realized that, while he was reluctant to infiltrate and deceive the cult, a part of him looked forward to the challenge. This was the sort of work he taught his investigative journalism students. Now, in addition to McPherson's objectives, he had a unique opportunity to take concepts from the theoretical realm and apply them to a real, undercover mission.

As instructed, he checked into the St. George Hotel, which turned out to be a rustic wooden building in the downtown area. At the reception desk, he handed his credit card.

"That won't be necessary," a white-haired, middle-aged woman smiled at him. "I know you're on your way to Bishop's land, and we have arrangements with them."

"Thank you very much," Michael said as she handed him a key.

"You know," the lady added, "Charles Bishop is a dear friend and hero of mine. There's nobody in this town who doesn't admire him."

Michael nodded and smiled at her. Stewart was right, he thought, the authorities around here would be very reluctant to act against a hero and a benefactor.

He left his suitcase in his room and stepped out for a stroll. Walking along the waterfront of the Puget Sound, Michael enjoyed observing the majestic mountains in the distance. He liked his anonymity. Nobody knew who he was, and nobody judged him. He wondered if he'll have time for himself on the Bishop's estate. As it was getting dark, he entered a café, where he had a light supper of salad and fresh bread, and went to sleep early.

On the following day, he received an early phone call from an unidentified number.

"Hello, Michael?"

"That's me," Michael said, not recognizing the male voice.

"My name is Ron. I'm running some errands in town, and I'll be at the hotel 'round ten o'clock to pick you up."

"Sounds good," Michael said. Glancing at his watch, he saw that he had enough time to grab something to eat and get organized.

He was waiting in the hotel's small lobby when Ron arrived. About five inches taller than Michael, the man's long black hair, thick beard, and band shirt contrasted heavily with the hotel's deep-country aesthetics. "Peace be with you, brother," he said to Michael as he shook his hand.

"Peace be with you as well." Michael didn't know what else to say. The man's grip nearly crushed Michael's fingers.

Ron released him and led him to a shiny, black Chevy SUV that looked new. Michael had no problem finding space for his belongings, and he sat in the comfortable front passenger seat.

"We have a long ride ahead of us," Ron said. "It ain't so far away, but the roads around here aren't exactly what you'd call freeways." Ron's voice was a little high-pitched for his gruff appearance, and Michael detected a minor southern accent.

They went down narrow and winding paved roads, but the ride itself wasn't too bumpy, as the roads were well maintained, and the truck was suited for the terrain.

"It's quiet on the land these days," Ron said.

"Isn't it always quiet out in the country?" Michael wondered.

"Well," Ron said, smiling tightly, "when everyone's around, we number about sixty people, not including kids. It can get a bit hectic."

"And not everyone is around?" Michael asked.

"Most folks are already on their way to Jerusalem. We're operating with a skeleton staff who stayed behind to attend the land, the kids, animals, and, of course, to take care of Charles."

"Charles isn't going to Jerusalem?" Michael asked.

"He can't. You know he was badly injured in Iraq. Normally, his condition doesn't stop him from fulfillin' his tasks, but such a trip could be a bit too much for him. Mostly, he doesn't want his presence to be a burden for the people who'd be doing God's holy work. He will supervise the whole operation from his command center on the land, and that, my friend, is where you come in."

"Where I come in?"

"Sure. As I understand it, Charles brought you in to be a spokesman. Your task is obviously very important, as you'll have to explain to the world what we did and why."

Michael nodded and wondered if he was up to the task.

"I'll be honest with you," Ron continued as he smoothly rounded a sharp turn. "I was against the idea of bringin' an outsider for such a delicate job. I know you teach at a prestigious university back east, and you have a way with words. Now, I also see that you're quite presentable. Still, I thought the job should have been given to the pretty lady, because she's one of us, and she's one hundred percent trustworthy."

"You mean Mary?"

"Of course, I don't have anything personal against you, only that you are a newcomer, unlike many of us who'd been with Charles for many years. We do get new people every now and then, but they don't always turn out to be the cream of the crop, if you know what I mean. For some reason, we attract weirdos."

For some reason? Michael thought to himself. *If you were not striving to bring about a world war that would kill millions, perhaps you wouldn't attract so many weirdos.*

"Have you known Charles long?" Michael asked. He couldn't agree with the mission he was to serve as a spokesperson for; however, he appreciated Ron's candor.

"We grew up in the same town in Texas, so I know what an exceptional human being he was already in his childhood.

There's nothin' I wouldn't do for this man," Ron lowered his voice and added, "I mean *nothin'*." He met Michael's eye for an instant before turning back to the road, and Michael's breakfast roiled in his stomach unpleasantly.

"I sure hope, Michael," Ron continued, "that you'll fit in and that Charles' decision to bring you on board will prove to be the right one. However, let me give you a friendly warning: don't even think of crossing us."

Chapter 24

Jerusalem 70 AD

My name is Elisha Ben-Shimon. I am a fifty-year-old man, and I've been a slave here in Rome for most of my life. I'm old and tired. I think it won't be long before I die and join my ancestors from the land of Judea.

My first master was a good man: he allowed me to learn to read and write Latin so that I could serve him better. After he died, I was sold to another master who was not so kind to me. He whipped me with a scourge for punishment, even when I had done nothing wrong.

But I don't wish to spend my last days on earth complaining. I want to write my memories of those horrific days, so many years ago, when the Romans came and demolished Jerusalem and destroyed and burned our holy temple. I hope these writings will survive so that people living in the future will know what happened, and how cruel, merciless, and barbaric the Romans were.

I must have been about nine or ten years old, the oldest of three siblings. I was very young and didn't understand everything, but I know what I saw. I remember that we, the Jews, rebelled against the mighty Roman Empire. My father said that it was a mistake. He was an expert shoemaker, and my mother was a seamstress. We were poor, but we had our own house in the upper section of Jerusalem, and there was never a shortage of food in our home.

Over four or perhaps five years, the Romans failed to suppress the uprising. But then one morning, we got up and looked outside the city walls and saw a huge army. They marched in straight lines as they got closer and closer. I know now that there were about sixty thousand Roman soldiers led by the Roman emperor, Titus. But back then, I knew only that there were so many of them, marching with their war machines, that I was engulfed by fear, and I knew that only a miracle could save us.

"If only we hadn't wasted our resources on internal wars," I remember my father saying. My father was uneducated, but he was a smart man, no less than those so-called wise leaders of the fanatic factions who fought against each other. They brought our demise because they couldn't compromise.

The Jewish defending force was small, but they were willing to fight till their last drop of blood—which they did. The zealot factions had finally united against a real enemy, but it was too late.

It started in a promising way for the Jews. A surprising counterattack caused the Romans heavy casualties, and Titus was nearly killed. Later, the massive Roman army had the upper hand. Titus had many soldiers to sacrifice. For every soldier killed, he had many replacements. He had powerful catapult machines that blasted our positions with big, weighty rocks that weakened and opened holes in the fortified walls. Those bombardments shielded the Roman soldiers who were building dikes and getting close to our protected defense lines.

Jerusalem had three layers of walls. With mighty battering rams, they broke through the first wall to arrive at a neighborhood where they massacred everyone, including women, children, and the elderly. After a few days, they broke through the second wall. They continued to advance and kill everyone in their way. The third, most fortified wall was located in the Antonia, a castle that King Herod positioned in order to control the Temple Mount and the temple.

Titus calculated that if the Antonia fell, so would the temple, and that would break the spirit of the Jewish defenders and bring about the fall of the city.

From our house in the upper part of Jerusalem, we saw the dike that the Romans built leading to the Antonia. But then something happened that the Romans didn't foresee. Brave soldiers of my people, led by Yohanan mi-Gush Halav, dug a tunnel under the dike and then set it on fire. The dike collapsed, killing hundreds of Roman soldiers. A similar attack was executed by soldiers under the command of Simon bar Giora, and it also had a devastating effect on the Romans.

At that point, Titus was shocked. We hoped and prayed that he'd withdraw, but he had no such plan. Instead, the Romans changed their strategy. In three days, they built a dike around the whole city, aiming to block our supply lines and starve us to death.

It worked. I remember how we were all so hungry. I couldn't fall asleep at night because my belly ached with hunger. The deprivation affected rich and poor, elders and children.

"The zealot factions," my father stated once again. "When they battled each other, they also burned their opponent's food supplies. If it weren't for their fanaticism, then we wouldn't be starving now."

Many people tried to escape Jerusalem, but the Romans caught most of them and crucified them outside the city walls. It made for chilling scenery. I remember turning to God and asking why he allowed such evil to be victorious. I also remember my father saying, "That's what they did to Yeshua." But I didn't know who Yeshua was.

Fatigue and hunger affected the defenders, but they still fought with everything they had. They shot burning arrows at the Romans, threw heavy rocks at the soldiers who climbed the wall, and poured hot oil on the invaders. After fierce fighting, the Romans conquered the Antonia castle and demolished it.

When our people saw that the temple was in danger, they forgot about their hunger and weakness. Everyone, including the old and the young, rushed to fight for the temple. Thousands of citizens, everyone who could hold a weapon, including my father and my mother, joined in defense of our holiest place of worship. That was the last time I saw my parents. I told them that I could fight next to them, but my mother said I was too young, and my father said, "Don't even think about it." In the years that followed, I reflected upon that moment many times, and wondered if I wouldn't have been better off if I'd joined the defenders and died in that fighting.

It was the ninth day of the Jewish month of Av. From my window, I saw the beautiful floor outside the temple flooded with blood and piled with dead bodies.

Then the Romans burned the temple. I heard that the traitor, Josephus, claimed that Titus forbade them to destroy the temple because he thought it was the most magnificent building he'd ever seen. Still, one of his soldiers misunderstood the order, threw a torch, and the temple went up in flames. I don't believe that story.

Then, the Roman soldiers went from one house to another, and eventually, they made it to our home. I told my little brother and sister to hide. Unfortunately, my sister was so terrified, she started to cry, and the soldiers heard her and found us. I was old enough to be put to work as a slave, but the Romans knew my siblings were too young to survive the long, hard journey to Rome. So, they slaughtered them with their swords right in front of my eyes.

Oh, how I hate the Romans. In my long years of slavery, I never stopped praying to God to destroy Rome for what they did to me, to my family, to my country, and for burning and razing our holy temple. Now I'm old and ready to die, and I still don't understand why God allows this evil empire to thrive.

Over the years, I've met slaves from many countries: Egypt, Arabia, Africa, Britain, Gaul, Germania. What the Romans did to us they did to other countries. Why couldn't we all unite to annihilate and erase this horrible and sinful empire from the face of the earth?

I have to stop writing because my master is calling my name. If I don't respond promptly, I will face a painful punishment.

Elisha Ben-Shimon.

Chapter 25

The SUV slowed down as Ron drove next to a tall metal fence. He stopped in front of a gigantic gate comprised of tall metal poles supporting two bulky, ornamented metal doors. Above the gate, a banner in old English proclaimed: *God's Land*.

"This is it," Ron said. He beeped the horn once and rolled down the windows, in no visible hurry.

After a few quiet minutes, the massive gate opened, and a young man approached the car.

"Hey, man," he smiled at Ron. "Where have you been?"

"I went to Olympia to run some errands and pick up Michael, our new volunteer."

"Greetings, brother," the young man smiled at Michael, "I'm David."

"Glad to finally be here," Michael said to David, who was dressed casually and had long blond hair tied in a ponytail and a light-colored beard.

"I didn't expect to see you at the gate," Ron said to David.

"Well, you know," David said, "a lot of people are away. Besides, I like to take breaks from the computer."

"David is a computer wizard," Ron told Michael as he drove past the gate.

About a hundred yards from the gate was an old wooden house. Ron kept driving slowly, bypassing the house. Behind the house was an old barn, and Ron kept driving down a winding, paved road that snaked up a hill. Michael saw various structures of different shapes and sizes. Some looked modern, while others seemed more temporary and improvised. Cabins, dome-shaped dwellings, yurts, and teepees all basked within a beautifully maintained landscape that combined wild and garden plants.

Ron stopped the car in front of a small wooden cabin. "This will be your place while you're here," Ron said. "It's quite comfortable and has heating and air conditioning. You'll find the kitchen small, but that doesn't matter since we eat most of our meals in the communal dining room. Make yourself comfortable in there." Ron checked his wristwatch. "You already missed lunch today, so grab yourself something from the fridge. In about an hour, Mary will pick you up, and she'll take you to meet Charles."

"Thank you, Ron, for everything," Michael said as he got out of the car and collected his belongings.

"You're most welcome," Ron said and drove away.

Michael took a long look at his surroundings. As soon as the car was no longer within hearing range, silence prevailed. All he could hear was the sounds of the burbling stream a few yards away, the wind sighing through the trees, and the birds.

The cabin appeared comfortable and homey, and Michael liked the atmosphere of a wooden dwelling. The place contained one large room with adjacent small bedroom, kitchen, and bathroom. Just like Ron said, Michael found some food in the refrigerator, and he made himself a cheese sandwich. The weather was pleasant—no need for heating or cooling—so, he just opened the windows.

Around 1:00 PM, he heard a knock on the door.

It was "the pretty lady," as Ron called Mary Bishop. Michael had a hard time defining her beauty, which was a bit enigmatic and alluring.

She wore a blue, embroidered shirt—that Michael recognized as a South American import—over a black skirt. Her long hair hung down in a braid and rested on her right shoulder. She wore her wedding ring.

"Hi, Michael," she said. "How do you like your stay here in *God's Land*?" She had a deep and pleasant voice, which Michael recognized from their online meetings.

"So far so good," he answered. "I have no complaints."

"Come," she said, "I'll take you to meet Charles."

When he stepped outside, he saw that Mary came with what looked like an open golf cart. The vehicle had one seat next to the driver and space for two or three more people in the back. He sat next to her, and she drove up the hill.

A light breeze fluttered their hair, and Michael forced himself to look away as the wind flipped Mary's skirt up, exposing the smooth, tan skin of her thighs.

"Are you from South America?" Michael knew it wasn't time for small talk, but he was curious.

"Most people think I am when they first meet me," she said. "My mother is Dutch and my father is Puerto Rican."

"I wondered about the blue eyes," he said.

She didn't respond and focused on driving until she pulled into the small driveway of a modest, one-story house. It looked just a little bigger than most of the other dwellings.

"Let's go," she said. Michael followed her up a wide sidewalk lined on both sides by large shrubs. She entered the house and Michael trailed behind her.

"Charles!" she called. "Michael is here!"

The house appeared pleasant, clean, and well maintained. Large windows allowed plenty of light, which was probably beneficial for the sizable house plants. There were very few decorations on the white walls. Michael noticed a large, hand-carved, wooden crucifix and one unusual mandala. Michael had seen oriental mandalas before, but this one had a cross at the center along with other Christian images, rather than Buddhist or Hindu symbols.

Within a short time, Charles Bishop rolled in on his wheelchair. Although Michael already talked with him face-to-face, online, meeting him in person was a different experience. Michael thought that Bishop conveyed splendor.

His surprisingly youthful face seemed to glow in the ample sunlight pouring into the room, and the smile he gave Michael was like being welcomed home after years on the road. His gentle eyes were bright with intelligence and compassion, and his expression was so open and sincere, that, for a moment, Michael felt as though he could unburden himself of every mistake, every sinful thought, without fear of judgment or rejection. Now he understood why everyone who knew the man admired him, and why there were those who were willing to follow him, even when the road he led them down was questionable.

"Praise be to God, you finally made it over here," Bishop smiled warmly.

Bishop's gaze was compassionate, but penetrating, as though he could see right through Michael.

Bishop extended both his hands and Michael grasped them, sensing that Bishop's grip was firm and steady.

"Praise be," Michael replied, and once again, he was perplexed, not sure how to answer the greeting.

Thank God, Michael thought. *At least his upper body is healthy and strong.* He realized how quickly he'd been charmed by Charles Bishop.

Chapter 26

Take these articles and go and deposit them in the temple in Jerusalem. And rebuild the house of God on its site.
-   ***Old Testament, Book of Ezra***

"Come, young man," Charles Bishop said. "Let's not waste our time."

Bishop, Mary, and Michael headed for the golf cart which had a specialized, electric ramp to accommodate Charles' wheelchair. Michael moved to the back of the vehicle, and the original front seat folded away.

Mary drove the all-electric vehicle up the mountain on a narrow, winding road. The paved section of the way ended when they reached the summit where Michael had only a moment to relish the beautiful scenery of the valley below. Mary continued downhill, driving into a forested area that stood in sharp contrast to the mostly open sky that Michael had met until that moment. They progressed under tall pine and Douglas fir trees, accompanied by the crackling sounds of dry needles crushed under the vehicle's wheels and occasional bird calls.

In an abrupt transition, they exited the forest and crossed into a large flat clearing. And there it was, erected in a vast, green meadow, towering over them in all its glory: the temple.

Though Michael had already seen the structure on-screen—before and after his online meetings with Bishop—he still gaped as he took the building in. Constructed in marble, gold, and white sandstone, the temple reminded Michael of an ancient Egyptian palace. Fortified on all sides by crenellation as grand and dazzling as the temple itself, the temple's rectangle heart speared the cloudless sky, supported by gold-tipped marble columns.

Gazing at one of the most magnificent structures he'd ever seen, Michael uttered the only word that came to his mind: "Wow."

As inconceivable as it may have seemed, Michael thought that he was looking at an accurate replica of the Temple of Solomon, not a miniature version as he had seen on some internet sites.

"Does it have the same measurements as the original?" Michael wondered.

"It does," Bishop answered, taking in Michael's expression with a satisfied grin. "We constructed it according to the *exact* measurements from the design of Sir Isaac Newton. Those measurements are found in his book, *The Chronology of Ancient Kingdoms,* and in other sources—including unpublished manuscripts. Newton spent a lot of time figuring the precise proportions of the temple. He thought that the temple had to be resurrected as a central pretext to the second coming of Jesus Christ. My vision is the execution of Newton's theoretical concepts."

"That's incredible," Michael said. "This temple ... it must have cost a fortune."

"A small fortune, yes," Bishop confirmed, "and a lot of hard work by my people. But, we did it with love and faith in order to fulfill God's plan for us and all true believers."

McPherson was right when he said that Bishop is obsessed with the temple, Michael thought.

"Charles," Mary said as she pulled onto the side of the path that led to the temple, "would you like to get off the vehicle?"

"Yes, my dear," Bishop answered with a loving glance at her.

Using the electric ramp, Mary lowered Bishop's wheelchair to the ground, then she walked toward the temple and disappeared inside.

Michael jumped from the back seat and joined Bishop. He felt uncomfortable standing next to him, being so much taller than the older man in the wheelchair, so he sat on the grass beside the wheelchair.

"What are you going to do with the temple?" Michael asked.

"This temple will stay here in *God's Land* and serve our community," Bishop said. "Essentially, we've built this shrine as a prototype and a practice model."

"Practice for what?"

"For the real temple, of course," Bishop said patiently, "which will be the third holy temple of our Lord. It will stand on the Temple Mount in Jerusalem."

"You have another temple?" Michael asked, baffled.

"We sure do," Bishop confirmed. "Most of my people are already in Jerusalem, putting my plan into action."

"But how is that possible?" Michael asked. "I admit I don't understand the plan. As far as I know, there's a Muslim structure, the Dome of the Rock, sitting right where the two Jewish temples used to be, on top of the foundation stone. To resurrect the temple in its original location, you'd have to remove, or perhaps blow up the Dome of the Rock. Is that the plan?"

Bishop smiled kindly at Michael and looked into his eyes like a father to a son.

"You are right about one thing," Bishop said. "For the prophecy to work, we indeed have to construct the temple in the original location of the old temples. However, we may not have to remove or destroy the Dome of the Rock, as we can build our temple right next to it—on the *true* location of the Hebrew temples. You see, plenty of evidence suggests the Muslims had built their shrine in the wrong place ..."

"The wrong place?"

"About two hundred yards from where the original, true temple of God stood."

"How is that possible?"

"History teaches us," Bishop explained patiently, "that when the Muslims first conquered Jerusalem in the year 638 AD, they didn't know where the Jewish temple had once stood. Hundreds of years had passed since the destruction of

158

the temple by the Romans. The Jews were not allowed to rebuild their temple, and the original site had become a dump.

"So, a Jew who converted to Islam pointed out the place for the Muslims. We know that many Jews converted to Islam at that time, but they didn't do so willingly and wholeheartedly. Most of them were forced to convert either through threats of persecution or by facing economic sanctions if they didn't comply. I find it likely that this Jew was also forcibly converted, and believe he took revenge at the Muslims by pointing them to the wrong location—about two hundred yards from the right place."

"It sounds like speculations to me," Michael said.

"I'm glad to find that you have an inquiring mind, just as I thought," Bishop said. "I do not wish to be surrounded by yes-men. I want my people to be motivated by deep conviction, not blind faith. The real location of the temple and the site of the foundation stone have been debated over the centuries by Christian theologians and Jewish religious leaders, and there are plenty of indications that point to what I've just said. Among those scholars, you could find the Rambam, who was one of the greatest Jewish mystics and thinkers of all time, and the modern researcher, Dr. Asher Kaufman. They use different sources and calculations to assert their conviction that the Dome of the Rock is not where the holy temple used to be. This is important, because according to the Old and New Testaments, without knowing the precise location, a new temple can't be rebuilt."

"So, what was the precise location of the old temple?" Michael asked.

"On the Temple Mount," Bishop said. "Around two hundred yards northwest of the Dome of the Rock, there is a small cupola called the Dome of the Spirits, or Dome of the Tablets. It's an interesting name, considering that the tablets of the ten commandments were kept in the Holy of Holies."

"Is it a place that people could visit?" Michael asked.

"Yes," Bishop answered. "The Muslims are very protective of the Dome of the Rock, and only allow people of their faith to visit it. However, they don't regard the Dome of the Spirits as very significant, which is why whenever tourists are allowed at the Temple Mount, they can visit the Dome of the Tablets."

"Have you been there?"

"Yes, I visited the Temple Mount before my injury. It's a fascinating place."

Michael looked at Bishop, whose eyes gleamed with hope despite all that they must have seen in his time. The man had accomplished so much and hadn't let his disability break his spirit or slow him down.

"I've read," Michael said, "that according to Jewish belief, the third temple should descend from the sky."

"My concern is not necessarily with satisfying the Jewish belief," Bishop replied, "but with setting the right conditions for the return of our Lord, Jesus Christ. Having said that, we are doing whatever we can to fulfill the ancient prophecies, including the Jewish ones; consequently, the temple will, in fact, descend from the sky."

Michael examined Bishop, to make sure he is not joking.

"We'll bring most of the parts in by helicopters," Bishop continued solemnly, "and assemble them on the ground in one night. It will be an enormous operation, and as challenging as this task could be, I trust that my people will rise to the occasion. Don't forget that they all have plenty of experience acquired while building this majestic shrine." Bishop looked affectionately at the temple.

"And what about the Israelis who now control the Temple Mount?" Michael asked. "I doubt that they'll allow such an operation. Actually, I'm quite certain that they'll intervene to block it."

"Michael," Bishop smiled and looked pleased, "You're asking all the right questions. As far as the Israelis are concerned, you're right. Although I'm sure that most of them would love to see the holy temple once again reigning on the Temple Mount, they could not allow such an operation to take place. After all, they are a small country, and the Muslims have 1.8 billion people."

"So?" Michael prompted, leaning forward and listening intently.

"The Israelis will be paralyzed and unable to do anything about our operation!"

"Paralyzed?"

"Yes." Bishop nodded. "Without any means of communication and with most electric power temporarily shut off. Do you remember the recent, unexplained computer freezes that virtually paralyzed our country and some European countries?"

"You were behind it?" Michael remembered that McPherson suspected Bishop right from the start, while the US authorities were helpless and without any clue as to who was behind it.

"Those shutdowns were tryouts," Bishop said. "We were testing our capabilities, and now we're confident that we can

162

count on our systems and technologies. However, we won't leave Israel in a defenseless, vulnerable state that could subject them to an enemy attack. So, we'll bring down most systems of power and communications all over the Middle East, while allowing emergency services to continue to function unhindered."

"Where will you get all the building materials, not to mention helicopters and pilots?" Michael asked, even though by then, he was starting to realize that Bishop had all aspects of the plan well thought out.

"While the Israeli government and armed forces implement neutrality over the holy sites," Bishop answered, "there are Jewish religious leaders whom we secretly contacted and who have already offered assistance, mainly in supplies and transportation. I requested that they not get involved in the actual construction of the temple and leave that task to my people."

"You're not concerned that, with so many people involved, the information could leak to the Israeli security services who would intervene and stop you?"

"That's a risk I had to take," Bishop nodded. "However, all my people are wholly devoted and committed to the mission. As far as our Israeli partners, I was assured that we are only collaborating with a selected group of fine people who are devout believers and passionate about our cause of rebuilding the temple."

"I still see a serious problem with the plan," Michael said, furrowing his brow as he considered all the flaws. "Even if we manage to build the entire temple overnight—next to the Dome of the Rock and not instead of it—the Muslims are unlikely to accept it. They might be stunned at first, but sooner or later, they *will* call for a holy war, aimed at removing what they would surely consider an abomination."

"And that's where you come in, my friend." Bishop smiled at him, having noted Michael's use of "we" rather than "you." It indicated acceptance and solidarity with his cause. "You'll have to explain and defend our action, and it won't be an easy task. It will require your proven academic skills and your ability to articulate your vision clearly and coherently.

"In a press conference that we will convene after our operation, you will tell the Muslims and the entire world that we come in peace. As I see it, Michael, the whole world will watch you, and that will certainly be your defining moment."

Michael realized that not only did Bishop think about every aspect of his plan, he had also meticulously calculated Michael's role in the process.

"I have to be honest," Michael said, "and tell you that it would be a challenging undertaking." He took his time to ponder the situation, aware that Bishop was examining him. "Now that I have a better picture of my responsibilities, I can see that it would require thorough preparation on my part." He wondered if he had the qualifications for such an immense task, that is, even without the significant matter that he came in as a spy, and thus, might be reluctant to present Bishop's standpoint.

"You know what could contribute to a successful presentation?" Michael had an idea.

"Tell me, I'm curious," Bishop said.

"Perhaps our perception of Islam as a militant religion is one-sided and prejudiced. It would be great if we could recruit an ally from within the Muslim world. A moderate religious leader who would appeal for calm and call upon the Muslims to accept the temple as a peaceful neighbor on the Temple Mount."

"I like your creative thinking," Bishop responded. "However, I'm highly skeptical we could find such a person in the short time that we have. After all, the man you're suggesting is likely to face a troubled community, including radical extremists who would consider him a traitor."

And how would these extremists consider me? Michael wondered. *Wouldn't they see me as a target?*

Bishop contemplated for a short while. "You know what?" he said to Michael, "I'm going to take a closer look at your idea. Perhaps we could find and recruit a moderate religious leader from within the American Muslim community."

"It's worth a try," Michael said.

Michael noted that when talking about the two courses of action—blowing-up the Dome of the Rock, or building the temple next to it—Bishop didn't use definitive language. He said his followers *may not* blow-up the Muslim shrine, but didn't commit to that option.

Chapter 27

"Please get Mary," Bishop bade Michael. "It's time to go."

Michael nodded and walked to the temple. He knew it was just a replica, a model that Bishop and his community created as a prototype; but, still, it was an enormous endeavor and a great accomplishment. Above all, it wasn't a replica of some insignificant building; it was the holy temple constructed according to the precise calculations of none other than Sir Isaac Newton.

Michael's heart pounded when he walked through the majestic entrance. It was dim inside, and it took some time for his eyes to adjust.

Michael wondered whether he would encounter the same meticulous attention to details in the inner part of the temple as he saw on the outside. Had Bishop and his people completed all the sections of the temple? The altar, the court of the priests, the Holy of Holies? That would have been an even greater achievement.

Michael entered a large rectangular hall, but it was too dark inside to distinguish many details. He would have to return some other time, during daylight, if he wanted to get a better idea of the inner shrine.

Looking for Mary, he wandered on, peering into every alcove, every shadow. Where could she be inside this vast space? Outside, the setting sun emitted a few last rays, and inside it was almost completely dark.

I wish I had a flashlight to see this place better. Or maybe an oil lamp would be more appropriate? Michael recalled a story he heard from his father-in-law, who was half-Jewish. In ancient times, people had lit an oil lamp in the temple, which was supposed to burn with an eternal flame. One time they nearly ran out of oil, and only one little pot remained with enough oil for one day. Miraculously, the oil lasted eight days. Michael couldn't remember much more detail nor why they had been reduced to only one small pot of oil. It happened during wartime, but he didn't remember whom they fought against. *Wasn't there always a war over there?*

At the center of the hall, he saw Mary's outline just in time to avoid bumping into her. *I've already looked here,* he thought to himself. *How come I didn't see her?*

168

"Mary," he said gently.

She didn't move. Sitting in an upright posture, she resembled a dark statue.

"Mary," he said again, louder this time. His voice echoed throughout the marble hall.

She didn't move.

The last golden sunray penetrated the building and briefly illuminated her face. *She is so beautiful*; he couldn't help but think. Another realization hit him: there was something about her that resonated within him and prompted him to reflect on another Mary, the Madonna he'd seen in so many paintings, the mother of Jesus.

"Miriam," he called softly, using the Hebrew name of the Madonna, and the name Mary used on the internet site. She trembled, and then slowly turned in his direction.

"Michael," she said, apparently recognizing his voice. "How long was I here?"

"A while," he answered. "We have to go, Charles is waiting."

"Oh, yes, Charles. We shouldn't make him wait." She extended her hand toward him.

He took her hand and helped her stand. Her tender touch made him tremble. Mary didn't pause before releasing his hand and heading for the gate.

Michael wondered if the temple should have inspired a certain sacredness within him. He thought he ought to return to the place when he had more time.

Chapter 28

Michael liked communal life at *God's Land*. The estate was largely self-sufficient. They had sizable organic fields where they grew most of their vegetables, a small lake where they cultivated fish, and a water purifying station. They also generated a portion of their electricity, utilizing renewable energy sources—like solar panels and wind turbines.

Michael missed his wife and daughter; but, most of the time, he kept busy with work and study which made it easier to accept his new circumstances.

Since many of Bishop's followers were in Jerusalem, there was a workforce shortage on the estate. Michael was assigned to work in the vegetable gardens, where he spent long hours under the hot sun and in occasional rain. Working outdoors was a new experience for him. Although the work was mostly monotonous and even boring at times, Michael found that he enjoyed the physical labor. Weeding around the vegetables, he had to get his hands dirty with the moist soil, and he liked being close to Mother Earth. He recognized that he was more mentally relaxed while working on the land, than at his regular teaching job, where he only exerted his intellectual capabilities.

His supervisor and guide was Ruth, an energetic, stocky woman with a chubby face and a very short hair. Always dressed in baggy clothes, she wore no makeup, and Michael had the impression that she cared little about her appearance. Ruth was funny at times, passionate, and vocal in her opinions.

"I used to be a JAP." She once told him and looked amused.

"JAP? What does that mean?"

"A Jewish American Princess," she laughed. "I looked quite different in those days. I believe I was cute."

"What brought you here?" He was genuinely curious.

"About ten years ago, I volunteered to serve in the Israeli army. At the military recruiting base, I said I wanted to be a fighter and not waste my time in a desk job, and they approved my request. The training was rough, physically and mentally, and my body ached by the end of each day, but I didn't complain. I had to show them I could do everything the guys did. I admit I liked the firing range. I liked every kind of weapon."

172

"You still like guns?" Michael asked.

"Definitely," she said. "Anyway, at the end of basic training, we were taken to an oath ceremony, where we had to pledge allegiance to the state of Israel. At that time, I didn't mind it, but I was seriously bothered by the location of the ceremony."

"Why? Where was it?"

"In a large square, right in front of the Western Wall, which I've heard is also called the Wailing Wall. Oh, or the Kotel."

"Why did it bother you?"

"Because I sensed that the Kotel wasn't the real thing. I looked above the Wailing Wall and saw the golden cap of the Dome of the Rock. Deep inside me, I was infuriated and hurt because the Dome of the Rock stood on the foundation stone where the holy temple used to be, and the Wailing Wall was just a lame substitution. I thought it was an outrageous injustice — that one religion builds a shrine on top of another religion's most sacred place."

"You know," Michael said, "the Jews did just that, too. King David conquered the Jebusites and took it from them."

"Not true!" Ruth retorted fervently, with a passion that surprised Michael. "King David *bought* the place from them. They could have refused to sell!"

"So," Michael said, "that's what brought you over to Charles?"

"Eventually. To Charles and also to Jesus. You know, Jesus also got infuriated when he saw the temple being abused. That was when he lashed out at the money changers. Still, I finished my service with Israel before returning home to New York. I'm not a quitter."

Ruth taught Michael words and expressions in Hebrew, as well as Arabic. She thought it could come in handy when he went to Jerusalem.

"I would love to teach you how to fire a gun," she said, "but our people don't like the noise, and I respect that."

***

Everyone met in the dining room three times a day, except for Charles and Mary, who ate at their house. Occasionally, when Charles joined the meal, he led his people in prayer and Bible study; otherwise, mealtime was a lively gathering where people talked mostly about work and the estate's upkeep.

Michael liked the communal meals and soon grew used to the noise and bustle. He participated in and contributed to conversations, exchanging opinions on various routine issues like cultivating crops, raising children, and politics. He liked not having to prepare meals or wash dishes, aware that while he worked hard in the fields, someone else's job was to prepare the food.

"The media is brainwashing us," accused a person he didn't know who happened to sit at his table. "They want us all to think the same way, and there's no difference between Democrats and Republicans."

"There's some truth to the accusation that a few rich tycoons dominate the mainstream media," Michael said. "However, in our country, there are plenty of alternative channels. Even within mainstream media, we can find independent-minded opinions and brave reporters."

"Brave," someone else said. "But, are they being heard?"

"I think they are," Michael responded, "though not always in the front pages of newspapers or prime spots on TV."

Some of the people listening gave appreciative nods, while others cut him sidelong glances, apparently still deciding whether he was trustworthy.

*****

Ruth was proud of her ability to operate a tractor. She skillfully maneuvered the small John Deere, taking extra care not to run over plants while driving between rows. As generous as she was in her conduct with Michael, she never allowed him to set foot on the tractor, which she referred to as "my baby." Although Michael wanted to drive the green vehicle, he never asked for permission, as he realized she had her limits.

One hot, sunny day, Michael was working hard in the field, using a wide hoe to prepare a new vegetable bed. As he raked the hoe into the soil, someone screamed "BAM!" behind him. Michael whirled, nearly slapping Ruth in the face with the hoe.

"Michael," she said, "you should never let anyone sneak up on you like I did."

"I'm not a soldier," he said, clutching his chest with one hand and letting out a chuckle. "I'm just a nerd who teaches at a university."

"Now you *are* a soldier," she rebutted. "At least as far as I'm concerned, you are in the army of Christ."

"Ruth," Michael said, "don't forget that Jesus wasn't a soldier either. I believe he was a peace-loving man."

"In that incident with the money changers, he was not so peace-loving. He took action for what he believed was right," she argued. "Come, Michael, let's take a break. You look like you could use a cold drink of water."

"Sounds good to me," he said.

They made their way to a small grove of trees on the outskirts of the fields and sat on the ground, in a nicely shaded spot, where they passed a large water jug between them.

"Do you know," Ruth asked, "how many times Jerusalem is mentioned in the Bible?"

"I have no idea."

"Six hundred and sixty times in the Old Testament and one hundred and forty-six times in the New Testament." Ruth seemed proud to display her knowledge.

"So? Do these numbers have any significance?" Michael had already learned that Bishop's people were fascinated by numbers.

"Guess how many times Jerusalem is mentioned in the Muslims' book, the Quran," Ruth said.

"I haven't the faintest idea," Michael responded.

"Zero!" she exclaimed triumphantly as if she'd just won the only religious argument that mattered.

"Are you sure?"

"Absolutely."

"So, what does that mean?"

"You're supposed to be the intelligent one, Michael," Ruth said, wagging her finger at him. "Don't you see that Jerusalem and the Temple Mount are not that important to Islam?"

"It is possible," Michael said slowly, gauging her reaction, "that Jerusalem was not important to the Muslims at the time the Quran was written, but it became important in the centuries that followed."

"And you know what I think?" Ruth asked.

"What do you think?"

"I think we should blow up the Dome of the Rock!"

Alarmed, Michael reached for the water jug, to refresh himself and hide his expression. He wanted to say that her idea was crazy, but knew he could not jeopardize his cover.

"You know it would cause a war?" Michael finally asked.

"Of course, I do," she answered. "A war that was prophesied more than two thousand years ago. We would just be the catalyst for what is meant to be."

Michael nodded and looked around. He saw green fields, already carrying a generous bounty of fresh vegetables. In the distance, beautiful, majestic mountains touched the sky and bestowed a picturesque background scenery. Everything was so peaceful in *God's Land*.

Why couldn't these people be happy with what God has provided for them? Why are they such zealots that they want to set our world aflame?

"Michael," she examined him, "are you against the idea of blasting that abomination off the face of the earth?"

"I'm not sure," Michael shrugged his shoulders. "I think we should leave the decision to Charles." Michael tried to sound casual. He focused on a little weed that grew near his feet, extended his hand, and pulled it out—to avoid eye contact.

Chapter 29

*And he carried me away in the Spirit to a mountain great and high,
and showed me the holy city of Jerusalem coming down out of
heaven from God, shining with the glory of God. Its radiance was
like a most precious jewel, like a jasper, clear as crystal.*

- ***Book of Revelation***

Twice a week, Bishop held "Bible study." Although
attendance was not mandatory, most of his people chose to
participate. Like Michael, they liked listening to Bishop's
deep, pleasant voice as he explained and guided his assembly
through different aspects of the path. Michael found that even
though he wasn't always focused—especially when he was
tired after a long day of laboring in the field—he still enjoyed
participating in the meetings.

The group gathered in a hall in a central building used for
various activities. The compound contained a library and a
playground for kids, and it housed the computer center,

which was off-limits for most people. Michael saw that the hall could fit a much larger group; however, he liked the small, cozy, personal kinship that developed during the discourses, and he enjoyed the warm, supportive atmosphere that Bishop skillfully inspired.

Bishop sat in his wheelchair on an elevated dais, and Mary always sat next to him, focused and attentive. The group sat in front of them, some on chairs, while others preferred to sit on the soft carpet. Teachings varied from fascinating aspects of prophecy to familiar biblical passages.

Michael remembered that McPherson had asked for recordings of Bishop's talks, and the Bible study seemed like an excellent opportunity to fulfill that request. Rachel, McPherson's contact person, gave him a small device with which he could secretly record the talks; however, Michael thought that recording openly would be easier and less risky. So, he approached Mary and asked permission to record the Bible study sessions.

"For what?" she inquired.

"So that I can listen to the talks again and again. It will help me become more fluent with the materials and enable me to explain our mission more coherently."

"Let me consult with Charles," she said, her smile slipping. Her dark blue eyes roved his face, searching for something, before she continued, "He doesn't usually like to have his talks recorded, because he believes they should be listened to in the right place and time and not taken out of context. However, he might make an exception in your case, because we know you have to absorb a lot of material in a short amount of time."

The following day, Mary approached him, her face open and friendly. "Go ahead," she said, her smile bright, "Charles doesn't see a problem with your request; just please use the recordings for your personal use and don't distribute them anywhere."

Since he'd received permission, Michael opted to use the recording capabilities of his cell phone rather than the sophisticated equipment that Rachel had delivered. He thought the latter would look suspicious.

One evening, Bishop chose to interpret a section from the Book of Joshua. He used to assign the aloud readings to Mary, who, like her husband, had a deep and pleasant voice. She read:

Now the gates of Jericho were securely barred because of the Israelites. No one went out and no one came in. Then the LORD said to Joshua, "See, I have delivered Jericho into your hands, along with its king and its fighting men. March around the city once with all the armed men. Do this for six days. Have seven priests carry trumpets of rams' horns in front of the ark. On the seventh day, march around the city seven times, with the priests blowing the trumpets. When you hear them sound a long blast on the trumpets, have the whole army give a loud shout; then the wall of the city will collapse and the army will go up, everyone straight in.

Michael was curious as to what interpretation Bishop would give the tale of how the Israelites, led by Joshua, conquered the city of Jericho.

"This is a significant story," Bishop started. "Let's look at the numbers and see what we can learn. Each day, for the first six days, the Israelites, carrying the Ark of the Covenant, marched a complete circle around the city, and we know that a full circle makes 360 degrees. Six times 360 makes 2,160.

"Now, on the seventh day, we learn that God instructed them to encircle the city seven times. How much is seven times 360?

"Two thousand five hundred twenty!" Ruth called out loud.

"That is true, Ruth." Bishop smiled at her.

Ron gave Ruth a playful shove on the shoulder. The others shook their heads and rolled their eyes, smiling as well.

"Now, we'll continue a little more with numbers, so bear with me. Do you know what the meaning of the name of the city, Jericho, is in Hebrew?"

There was a pause of silence, as it seemed nobody would know the answer to such a question. "It has something to do with the moon," Ruth finally said.

"Thank you, Ruth," Bishop said. "I'm glad we have a Hebrew-speaking soldier among us."

Ruth beamed, clearly pleased.

"Now," Bishop continued, "by marching around Jericho's walls for six days, and encircling it for 2,160 degrees, the Israelites marked the moon's diameter in modern mile measurements."

Bishop paused. Everyone was quiet, trying to comprehend what he has just said.

While Bishop was silent, his voice continued to ring out in the large space, seeming to encircle all of them, as if his words were the only thing that existed at that moment.

184

"Could you clarify?" Mary asked quietly.

"Fine, Mary," Bishop said. "All you need to do is go to the internet and ask for the diameter of the moon. Last time I checked, I received an answer of 2,158.8 miles, which is definitely within the margin of error."

"This is amazing!" Mary said and looked appreciatively at her husband.

"Indeed," Bishop confirmed. "I want you people to realize that God created his world according to rules that he left for his most devout followers to decipher. Within these rules, Jerusalem, the temple, and the Ark of the Covenant take a central role. Sir Isaac Newton knew that, and now it's our turn.

"Before we go home," Bishop continued, "I would like to let you in on one more number." He paused and affectionately examined the group. "I hope you are not too tired to receive this information."

"We could sit here with you all night," said Roger, a man with whom Michael was briefly acquainted.

"Thank you, Roger." Bishop nodded in his direction. "Okay, people, does anyone knows what the diameter of Earth is?"

After a few seconds of silence, Ruth called out, "Seven thousand, nine hundred and seventeen-point-five miles."

Several people turned their heads toward her in surprise and appreciation.

"Very good, Ruth," Bishop smiled. "I see that you know how to access the internet on your smartphone. Now, people, Ruth said—and she is correct—that the diameter of the earth is 7,917.5 miles. Let's look at the calculators on our phones. How much would 2520 times pi be? Let me remind you that pi is approximately 3.14159."

Silence prevailed in the hall as people reached for their phones' calculators.

"This is incredible!" David proclaimed. Everyone knew that David was a computer genius who didn't require the use of a calculator.

"Fascinating," Roger said, glancing up at Bishop with awe-glazed eyes.

"I'm astonished," Ron echoed, shaking his head in disbelief.

"Unbelievable," Ruth said, her mouth popping open as she met Bishop's eyes.

"Oh, Ruth, in fact, it's very believable," Bishop said. "People, you are witnessing just a few of the clues that God left for his most sincere disciples."

Michael, who always opted to sit comfortably on a chair rather than on the carpet, followed the presentation attentively. Like everyone, he was amazed by the knowledge that Bishop shared. He also noticed that Bishop didn't need notes or a calculator to pull out his surprising numbers. However, something didn't sit well with Michael regarding Bishop's calculations. A fundamental problem needed clarification. Did he dare let his curiosity prompt him to pose the question? Or was it better to just sit quietly and not stand out as an outsider?

Apprehensively, Michael slowly raised his hand.

"Yes, Michael?" Bishop nodded in his direction.

"Like everyone here, I'm quite amazed," Michael said. "But aren't we mixing two unrelated eras? I mean, we're using units of measurement—like miles and pi—derived from our time, and imposing them on a completely different period. I'm quite certain that the ancient Hebrews who encircled Jericho used very different measuring elements. I'm sure they didn't use miles, which are imperial calculating units."

There was silence in the hall as an atmosphere of perplexity descended upon the group. Several members examined Michael, furrowing their eyebrows.

The awkward silence dragged on around Michael. Second after second, he felt the air growing heavier with each participant surveying his face. Michael's shoulders started to curve inward. He regretted asking the question as he hated to be the one spoiling the party.

"A great question, Michael!" Bishop warmly smiled at him. "People, I've asked Michael to join us because I thought we could benefit from his rational thinking and courage. I saw that he could point us to issues that our deep conviction may not allow us to see."

People nodded in agreement, but still appeared uneasy about Michael's challenge.

"So, first, I agree with Michael: the Hebrews didn't use miles. As far as pi is concerned, it was widely known among the wise sages of antiquity: Greeks, Egyptians, Babylonians, Persians, and also the Hebrews who just came out of Egypt.

"I have spent a considerable amount of time tackling the issue that Michael brought up. In my studies, I discovered a striking correlation between our modern forms of measurement—namely inches, feet, and miles—and the old

188

ways of calculating sizes, primarily the cubit used by the ancient Hebrews. It's late, and I don't want to tire you with unnecessary details. The important thing is that there is indeed a direct correlation, and so I'm sure that using the cubit system would have yielded similar striking results to those we've seen tonight. What's amazing is that three thousand years after God's messages manifested for the Hebrews, they are still alive, vibrant, and relevant for us, Christians of the twenty-first century." Bishop paused, looked into every open face, and smiled warmly.

"Praise be to God. Good night."

Chapter 30

Jerusalem 1099 AD

They were nine siblings in her Muslim family, four boys and five girls, and Fatima was the youngest.

Her best friend was the Jewish neighbors' daughter, Rivka. Both of them were born in the spring, eleven years earlier, with Rivka only a few days older than Fatima.

The two girls liked to play together on the streets of their city, Al-Quds, and they also liked to visit each other's house. While visiting Rivka's home, Fatima was fascinated by the different ways of life of her next-door neighbor. She saw how they lit candles every Friday evening to welcome the Sabbath, and she especially liked to observe the Jewish holidays.

"They have such nice holidays," she once complained to her mother. "Why don't we have some holidays, too?"

"But we do," her mother said. "We have two long holidays, or have you forgotten?"

190

"But it's not the same," Fatima argued. "Their holidays are so different, and each holiday comes with different foods and stories. They have a holiday when they all dress in costumes, and a holiday when they light candles, and a holiday—"

"Fatima, that's enough!" Her mother snapped. "It's time you start to appreciate what you have and how hard we work, so that you can run around and fill your head with all kinds of nonsense."

"I like the bread that they eat," Fatima said. "It tastes so good."

"In this house we eat pitas, your brothers and sisters like it, and it should be good enough for you!" Her mother turned away and continued with cooking the family's dinner.

Fatima knew that Rivka's parents had to pay heavy taxes because they were not Muslims. Rivka, however, never complained about it. Perhaps she didn't understand what it meant.

One time, when there were no grown-ups around, Rivka secretly told Fatima: "I heard my father saying that the name of our city wasn't always Al-Quds. He said that the Jews once ruled the city, and they had a great king named David, and the name of the city was Jerusalem."

191

"Nonsense," Fatima's father said when she asked him if it was true. "The Jews like to make up stories because they have a vivid imagination."

When Fatima was eight years old, she overheard her father discussing the events of the day in the grocery stand that he ran in the market.

"I'm worried, Abdallah," he told his friend. "There are rumors that the Christians are coming to fight us. They want to conquer our beloved Al-Quds and turn it into a Christian kingdom."

"I wouldn't get too concerned about it," Abdallah calmly answered while inspecting the figs on display. "You know that rumors tend to come and go; and, if those Christians ever get here, which I certainly doubt, then we'll fight them. You remember that they once held the city, and we captured it from them."

"Of course, I remember," Fatima's father said. "They ruled the city for three hundred years, and the Temple Mount became a garbage dumping ground. Now that we built our marvelous Dome of the Rock, they remember that the place is sacred for them."

"Let's not forget," Abdallah said, "that the prophet Muhammad visited the Temple Mount at night, riding on the back of the winged creature Buraq, and from there, he ascended into heavens where he received instructions from God."

"Today, unfortunately, we are divided and fighting among ourselves." Fatima's father said, his forehead crinkling as he rubbed the back of his neck. "That's why I'm so worried."

"Don't worry, Ahmed," Abdallah said. "With Allah's help, they won't even get here. It's a long journey from wherever it is that they come."

Fatima heard the discussion and tried not to think about it. *Let the grown-ups worry about such matters.*

A year later, when Fatima was nine and helping her father in his little store, she once again heard her father expressing his concerns to his friend.

"Antioch has fallen, Abdallah," her father said. "Do you still think a Christian invasion is just a passing rumor?"

"I don't know, Ahmed," Abdallah admitted, sadly shaking his head as he poked one of the fruits, checking for ripeness. "But what can we do? Worrying isn't going to help, you know. Besides, they are still far away. I heard that it's not a trained army that is heading our way, but mostly, an unholy

193

mixture of people. The leadership in their countries wanted to get rid of them, so they sent them in our direction. You know they are calling our city Jerusalem?"

"I heard this term from my daughter," Ahmed's smile was gloomy.

Two years later, the Crusaders arrived and besieged Al-Quds. Fatima heard their noise and ran up the dozens of stairs to look out through one of the embrasures and found the source of the commotion. A sea of red and gold lay just outside the city gates, line after line of enemy soldiers looking right back at her. They blew horns, announcing their presence, as they marched in an organized procession.

"What are they doing?" Fatima asked her father, who heard the horns and came to look at the unusual scene.

"I heard that they believe that if they circle the wall seven times and blow their horns, the walls will collapse."

"Will they collapse?" She felt like Her heart dropped into her stomach.

"Of course not," he said. "It's just an old tale from the Jewish Bible."

"Are they Jewish or Christians?"

"They are Christians, so they believe in the Jewish book and they also have their own book, which is mostly about Jesus."

She'd never met a Christian, and they scared her. If they'd been Jewish, she could have hidden in Rivka's house.

"Will they kill us?" She hesitantly asked her father.

He kneeled in front of her and looked into her eyes. "Sweetie," he said, "I can't lie to you and tell you that I know all the answers. But I know that Allah is the most powerful God. We must pray to him in this difficult hour so that he'll save us and help us defeat the infidels."

After her conversation with her father, she tried hard to follow his directions. She looked at the Crusaders through the firing slits in the wall, and then she closed her eyes and prayed. *Oh, Allah, the most powerful and merciful God, make them go away.* But when she opened her eyes, they were still there.

It turned out that her father was right. The Crusaders' attempt to bring down the walls using the biblical method failed. But then, they laid siege upon the city, with constant attacks on the city's already weakened fortifications—due to internal Muslim wars.

The Crusaders built tall siege towers, a battering-ram, and several catapults. After five weeks during which the defenders were subject to constant bombardments, the Crusaders broke through the walls and raided the city.

From her house in the upper section of the city, Fatima watched the Christians advancing through the streets. They seemed jubilant, even ecstatic, as they proceeded from house to house, massacring everyone in their path—soldiers and civilians, women and children, Muslims and Jews. Horrified, the eleven-year-old girl saw that the crusaders were making their way toward the Temple Mount, leaving behind them streets saturated with blood and piles of dead bodies.

Fatima bit back a sob as she curled up against her mother. They were huddled beneath the bedroom window, trembling with silent tears as they listened to the sigh of metal swinging through the air, and the crunch as it met flesh. The enemy soldiers laughed like hyenas as they burst through doors and dragged people outside. Fatima heard Rivka's mom pleading with a soldier only yards away. Then, there was the sound of the woman's last agonized cry as her body hit the ground. Through the window, Fatima, her face streaked with tears, raised her gaze to the dark, smoke-filled sky, and reached out one final time, *God, where are you?*

Chapter 31

Charles Bishop was not only the founder and spiritual leader of his organization, he was also a father figure. His people, many of whom came from broken families, knew that they could turn to him in a time of need, that he was available to listen, consult, and provide assistance. They knew that he truly loved them and cared about them, and they loved him as well.

Deeply trusting him, they had no doubt in their minds that they would follow him wherever and whenever he would lead them, and they would do just about anything for him.

Bishop used to conduct one-on-one consultations with his people. The sessions took place at his cabin, scheduled according to a list that Mary managed. Alternatively, people could request a meeting outside of regularly scheduled hours.

As could be expected, Michael also received his scheduled appointment—about two months after arriving at *God's Land*. Although it wasn't an out of the ordinary meeting, Michael felt quite nervous beforehand and worried about its outcome.

Alarm bells pealed in Michael's mind, warning that there was more to the meeting than a spiritual leader who wanted to become acquainted with a member of his community. *I shouldn't fall for his charm*, he told himself. *I must remain vigilant and not let my guard down.*

Pacing around his little cabin, Michael was keenly aware that the meeting could seal his fate, or at least seal the fate of his undertaking. If he were exposed as a spy, then all the efforts he'd devoted to the mission would have been in vain. He realized how invested he was in his objective and how strongly he identified with the idea that he must prevent a colossal war.

It was already dark when Michael made his way to Bishop's cabin. Feeling inadequately prepared, he wished he could consult with someone he trusted, perhaps with McPherson, or better yet, with the one person in his life who was incredibly smart and knew how to evaluate people and situations. The woman who was capable of looking deeply into the matter and separating the essential from background noise. Melany. He thought about her and felt a certain warmth in his heart, along with a sense of longing.

Just be yourself, he could hear Melany whisper.

Michael rang the doorbell, and it made a pleasant, chiming sound.

"Hello, Michael," Mary, opening the door, welcomed him. "Come in; we're waiting for you."

She wore a long, embroidered, white dress that beautifully emphasized her dark hair and brown body. Michael also smelled a touch of a pleasant perfume.

He followed her through a corridor into a large room and sat on the chair she pointed to.

"Would you like anything to drink?" Mary asked, playing her role as hostess. "We have a wide selection of herbal teas."

"Peppermint would be nice."

Mary nodded and exited the room.

Looking around, he deduced that he was in the living room. The relaxing sound of a flute playing near flowing water emanated from an invisible sound system. A woodstove emitted pleasant warmth against the evening's chill. Michael assumed that they got help in fueling the stove, since Charles Bishop obviously couldn't chop wood and he couldn't envision Mary wielding an axe.

Mary entered with a cup of tea on a small tray, which she placed on a wooden table next to him. She smiled and exited again. Michael assumed she went to help her husband get dressed.

There was a small jar of honey on the tray. He mixed a teaspoon of honey in his tea, took a sip, and leaned back in the chair. The room felt pleasant and homey. He wondered if his hosts wished they had children.

After several minutes, a door opened, and Charles Bishop rolled in on his wheelchair. Smiling, he extended his hand.

"Praise be to God," Bishop greeted as he shook Michael's hand. "You're the last one to join us so far, so we haven't had the opportunity to meet each other as we should have."

"I'm honored to be here," Michael shyly said.

"Please, son," Bishop said, "I'd like to get to know you better, so help me do that. Tell me about your upbringing."

A tingle raced up Michael's spine at the word "son." He took a deep breath, tried to get his thoughts in order, and said, "I had a normal childhood."

Did I really? an inner voice nagged.

"Go on," Bishop encouraged him.

"I grew up in San Diego."

Bishop nodded. His eyes shined.

There was something about him, Michael perceived, especially about his eyes that conveyed goodness, honesty, love…

"My mother was a teacher, my father …" Michael looked at Bishop, who listened attentively. "My father was …"

Bishop's face conveyed empathy and approval. Still, Michael sensed that despite the man's apparent acceptance of his words, Bishop saw through his lies.

Michael understood that not only was he being untruthful with Bishop, he was also dishonest with himself. Although what he told Bishop was true to an extent, it was only a partial truth and thus a lie.

Perplexed, Michael looked at Bishop, whose long gray hair and beard were combed and well-maintained. Bishop radiated utter compassion. He gently lifted his eyebrows and gave Michael an encouraging smile, signaling to Michael that he could continue. Michael couldn't pretend anymore.

"In fact, I was adopted. My biological mother was raped when she was sixteen. My father …" Unable to control his emotions, he started to weep. His body trembled. Then, he expressed it as he'd never done before, "I was born as a result of rape. My father took advantage of my mother, drugged, and raped her. I … shouldn't really be here."

202

"Of course, you should be here, and, thank God, you are," Bishop said, gripping the arms of his wheelchair and leaning forward to meet Michael's gaze. He held the stare, making sure Michael heard every strong, steady word. "It wasn't your fault, and you must not blame yourself. Come, Michael, let me hug you."

Michael kneeled in front of Bishop, allowing the man in the wheelchair to caress his head.

When Michael's body stopped trembling, he went back to his chair and tried to regain his composure. Through teary eyes, he saw Charles Bishop; his expression conveyed affection and tenderness.

"It's not for us," Bishop said, "to determine why God chooses to put us through certain lessons. One thing I know is that if we trust in our Lord, we learn to see that everything has a reason. We must not impose our presumptions of how our lives should be on the Lord's plan. Believe me, I've been there. I struggled with my disability so much that I even contemplated suicide. That was before I learned to surrender, trust, and accept that God has a special role for me and it's not what I dreamed of when I was a boy."

But I came here as a spy, and I don't deserve to be in God's Land!!! Michael wanted to say. He needed to say, to scream, to confess everything, to come clean, to have no more secrets. But instead, he said nothing, just letting the tears roll on his cheeks and down to his beard.

Walking home in the dark, Michael felt like he'd gone through a sublime experience. Now, he understood why Bishop's people loved him so much. Now, he loved him too. He wished he'd met Bishop under different circumstances in which he didn't have to conceal his real mission.

But how is it possible? The question burned inside of him. *How come such an immensely beautiful man is conspiring to bring the world to a horrible war? With such a kind heart and all his money and power, can't he do better things in the world than plotting the return of Christ—which is so unrealistic?*

Chapter 32

"The divine origin of the Bible is for Newton absolutely certain, a conviction that stands in curious contrast to the critical skepticism that characterizes his attitude toward the churches. From this confidence stems the firm conviction that the seemingly obscure parts of the Bible must contain important revelations, to illuminate which one need only decipher its symbolic language. Newton seeks this decipherment, or interpretation, by means of his sharp systematic thinking grounded on the careful use of all the sources at his disposal."

- **Albert Einstein. September 1940**

Although not all of Bishop's discourses were fascinating, Michael enjoyed other aspects of the meetings. He liked the atmosphere of community that Bishop had so elegantly developed, the sharing of hearts and minds, and the genuine caring for one another. But Michael didn't deny that watching Mary was his favorite part of these hours. He relished simply gazing at her as she sat beside Bishop, absorbed and attentive. *The Madonna*, he called her in the privacy of his thoughts.

Ever since his childhood as an adopted son, Michael wanted to belong, to be an integral part of a larger group. Yet, no matter how far he advanced in his career or how successful he became, in some hidden place deep inside his being, he always felt like an outsider.

He came to *God's Land* on a spying mission and found himself laboring long hours in the field, away from his beloved wife and daughter and his position at the university. Still, he couldn't deny that he experienced moments of sharing, of being part of something greater than him, which filled his heart with joy and gratitude. However, when he came to his senses, he remembered that, despite those moments of elation, he was the spy, an infiltrator, and definitely an outsider.

***

It was Sunday morning. Charles Bishop led his small congregation in a prayer of gratitude to the Creator. He reminded his people that they were living in a unique environment and were tremendously fortunate to be at a pivotal time when a new majesty was about to be born.

After the prayer, Michael packed a couple of sandwiches and a bottle of water into a small backpack and went for a hike on the vast estate. He walked past the green fields where he worked during the week, and where the group cultivated their crops, climbed grassy hills where wildflowers grew in abundance, crossed a creek via a small bridge, and took a break by the small lake. Breathing the fresh air, he relished the serene setting. The lake seemed like a good place for a break. So, Michael found a place to sit, and pulled a sandwich out of his backpack.

He recalled that when McPherson first told him about Bishop and his land, he thought it was surrounded by barbed wire fences and possibly armed guards. Michael didn't see any such protective measures in the peaceful environment. Perhaps the remote location was enough protection.

The sun reached its apex when Michael entered the forest. Walking at a leisurely pace, he savored the sound of the breeze passing through the treetops and the birds that called each other, perhaps warning their community of the intruder.

All at once, there were no more trees, as he exited the forest and stepped into a large meadow. In front of him stood the magnificent structure that he'd seen on his first day in *God's Land*, when he'd visited the place with Charles and Mary. The temple. Even though he'd seen it once before, it was still a breathtaking sight.

Michael wasn't sure whether he just stumbled upon the temple, or his subconscious directed his walk all along.

Slowly and hesitantly, he approached it. During his previous visit to the temple, he was absorbed in a conversation with Charles Bishop, but now he had a chance to observe and appreciate minor details. Two enormous golden pillars flanked the front of the temple. A pair of colossal, bi-folding doors—ornamented with golden, embossed cherubim, palm trees, and blossoming flowers—loomed over the stone courtyard. Could he just enter? Should he ask permission? From whom?

He took a deep breath, pushed the doors open, stepped inside, and closed the doors behind him. His heart pounded as he entered a large rectangular hall.

Natural light penetrated the high, narrow windows, illuminating the space. Wood-paneled walls created a warm interior, and several embellishments appeared similar to the decorations on the doors. There were ten large menorahs, five on each side of the room, but they were not lit. Stairs led to another large door in front of him, which he assumed was the entrance to the Holy of Holies. He decided not to enter that door, sensing that it could be interpreted as trespassing and a sign of disrespect.

Emitting a sweet fragrance, incense burned on a small altar—indicating that someone must have visited the temple shortly before him.

Since it was getting cold, he pulled a blanket from his small backpack, wrapped it around his body, and sat at the center of the vast hall. Michael didn't consider himself a spiritual person, and he never attended meditation classes or retreats. Still, being alone in the vast space, he sat cross-legged as it felt like the appropriate position for that moment.

Slowly, he closed his eyes.

Silence prevailed inside the temple—a different silence than Michael had ever experienced, as he only knew silence that stemmed from the absence of noise and turmoil.

The temple's silence felt powerful, vibrating with life. It was a silence that had … sound. It could have given rise to any sound that Michael had ever come across, and for a brief moment, he heard horns playing music in the distance.

As he sat with his eyes closed, he sensed his body being lifted and then floating above the ground. Was it due to the measurements and dimensions that Isaac Newton derived from the Bible? Or did his mind play tricks on him?

Fear crept into his mind, and he opened his eyes to make sure he was still sitting on the temple's floor.

He focused on regulating his breathing and attempted to relax. Long inhale, long exhale. After a few minutes, his breaths became slow and even, and his heartbeat slowed. His eyes felt heavy as they closed again, and his head drooped. Though he remained sitting, the world around him slowed and quieted, lulling him to sleep.

When he woke, he was still sitting. He raised his head and looked around to orient himself. He keenly saw the dream from which he just woke up. A dream or a vision? He wasn't sure. In the dream, he saw himself as a baby, right after birth. He lay upon his mother's bosom, curled within a loving embrace, and both of them drifted into a deep sleep. After several minutes, a nurse walked into the room, accompanied by a nun. Both of them stood beside the bed for a while, observing the sleeping mother and son. It seemed that the nun instructed the nurse to perform what they came to do. The nurse nodded in consent and swiftly pulled the baby from his mother's grip and took him into her own arms. Then the nun and the nurse walked out of the room with the sleeping baby. His mother didn't wake up.

He'd had that dream once before, but this time it was more vivid. The previous time had happened while he dozed in front of the television while watching a TV show called *The Broadcast*. Back then, he thought it was a vision, a message that pointed to the circumstances of his birth at a time when he was searching for his biological mother. This time the images were clearer and more memorable, and he wondered whether the message was different. How so? He wasn't sure, but perhaps, considering where he was—in the replica of the temple, a building and a concept coveted by so many people over the centuries—could the message be more universal?

Aren't we all removed from the bosom of our mothers after birth? And don't we spend our lives struggling to return to the source? To the garden of Eden? To be innocent again? To be as we were before

this world and this life corrupted us? And who removed the baby
from his mother? A nurse, true, but a nun instructed her...

Michael thought that the nun might symbolize organized religion. He remembered Isaac Newton's assertion that most religions had become corrupted over the centuries.

Suddenly, Michael was struck by an ambiguous sensation that he was not alone in the temple. There was another presence in the large hall, and the realization sent tingling throughout his skin. He cautiously looked all around. It was getting dark, so it took him some time to spot her. But there she was, sitting where he saw her the last time he visited the place. The woman whom, in his mind, he referred to as the Madonna.

Sitting erect with a blanket wrapped around her, she smiled at him.

"How long have you been here?" he asked.

"A while," she said. "I didn't want to disturb you. I know people come here to have visions. I often come here to receive guidance."

He contemplated her answer for a while. "Do you use the temple for communal events?

"Charles likes to use it only for special occasions. He doesn't want it to become a mundane place, so we use it for special ceremonies, major holidays like Christmas and Easter, and also for weddings and funerals."

"Funerals?"

"We haven't had many of those, thank God."

He was silent for a moment.

"You know," she said. "I'm not a Madonna …"

"What did you say?" He worried she read his mind.

"I'm more like Mary Magdalene than the Virgin Mary."

Michael peered into the deepening darkness and had difficulty reading her expression, even though she sat just a few yards from him. Still, even without visual contact, he had a strong sense of her presence, that magnetized him.

"Do you want a ride?" she asked. "I came here with our electric vehicle."

"Yes," he replied. "That would be nice."

They both got up. He started to head for the entrance, but she stood in his path and blocked his way.

"Mary?"

Instead of turning towards the door, she moved a step closer to him. He could sense her being, breathing next to him but not touching him. She smelled like the pines in the forest.

"Mary," he whispered. "If either of us were not—"

"Shut up, Michael," she said and moved towards him.

He opened his arms and accepted her in his embrace, knowing that his body yearned for her. They held each other, felt each other, inhaled and exhaled together as their breathing synchronized. He caressed her silky hair, resting his lips against her forehead.

For a few minutes, they stood in a loving embrace. In the stillness of the temple, they heard their hearts beat as one. She then took a deep breath and stepped away from him.

"It's getting dark," she whispered. "Let's go."

Chapter 33

Melany

I miss Michael. I miss his quiet presence. I'm angry at him for leaving, for taking a break in the middle of our lives—from Linda and me. And still, I miss him. I believed him when he said he had to go and save the world or whatever it was, but why did it have to be him, of all people? Aren't there other people? Authorities? The FBI? Isn't he playing the superhero?

I believe that he'll come back to me when this is all done, but naturally, I have my anxieties. What if he'll meet another woman? Another superhero? Michael is a decent and loyal person, but he's a man—a good-looking man. I see how women look at him, and I know he's not without weaknesses.

Linda needs her father. They have a special bond, and I can tell that she misses him very much. Sometimes, she misbehaves, refusing to do things, like going to sleep on time or taking a shower or eating vegetables. She is testing me and testing her limits. I try to be patient with her, but there are times when I lose my temper and shout at her and even grab her by the hand, take her to her room, and shut the door. She screams, of course, and says she hates me, which makes me feel awful. It happens especially when I'm loaded with work and have to prepare for a trial.

I hired a helper, Ashley, a twenty-five-year-old woman, to help around the house and with Linda, who seems to like her. Maybe Linda is angry at me for letting Michael go, or for not being able to hold on to him, and she doesn't have those issues with Ashley.

I also know I need a man in the house, which sounds selfish. Occasionally, I get scared. I think I'm even becoming a bit paranoid, and I imagine things. Every now and then, I get a strange feeling that someone is watching me. There were a few incidents when I noticed that the computer's camera was on, and I was sure I didn't turn it on myself. I hope I'm not losing my sanity. I questioned Henry about it, in an indirect way, but he didn't know what I was talking about.

Henry is patient and supportive; but, at times, our communication is tense. It happens when he realizes that I see him as a friend and not a possible new romance. Still, most of the time, we have a great connection. We understand each other and have fun and laugh together, which I need. Occasionally, he asks me about Michael, which annoys me; questions like, is he really a fanatic? And what's his job nowadays? When that happens, I gently change the subject. If he persists, I tell him I don't want to talk about it.

On weekends, I usually drive to my parents' home in Scarsdale, as it feels somewhat lonely staying home, just Linda and me. But over there, I sometimes feel that they pity me. I see it in their eyes, and that annoys me, too.

One time, shortly after I told my mother for the tenth time that I was confident Michael would come back to me, I overheard her telling my sister that I was in a state of denial.

Why is it that when a person has fallen on hard times, people like to patronize him? At times, I even think that they enjoy the situation because it gives them something to talk about: "Oh, poor Melany." They just don't know how strong I am and how strong the bond is between Michael and me.

Chapter 34

Every two weeks or so, Michael traveled to Olympia with Ron, who drove there regularly to run errands for the community.

As far as the group was concerned, Michael went to Olympia to take care of personal matters, like renewing his passport, shopping for clothes and shoes, or sending a gift to his daughter. However, the main purpose of the trips was to meet with Rachel. During those rendezvous, he delivered his recordings of Bishop and communicated information to and from McPherson.

They held their meetings in the back of a small café that Rachel picked. She was sure that it was a discreet location and that there were no cameras where they sat.

Michael could tell that Rachel liked him. It wasn't anything that she did or said, just how she looked at him, that reminded him of the high school girls and how they adored him—especially when he played his guitar. He liked her as well, but not in the same way. He found her to be an intelligent and cheerful young lady, and he hoped that anyone seeing them together would suspect a romantic connection, rather than anything to do with spying. Rachel always wore her blonde wig to their meetings.

"Sounds like your cult is obsessed with the temple," Rachel said when they met one afternoon, about three months into the investigation. She twirled her faked blond hair around her finger and added, "in that respect, they're no different from my sister in Jerusalem."

"You have a sister in Jerusalem?" Michael raised his brows at the unexpected information.

"She lives in the Jewish quarter of the old city as an Orthodox Jew."

"I didn't know you came from a Jewish family."

"I don't," she said, pouring cream into her coffee. "My family is Protestant, and I'm a complete atheist, especially after my older sister, Charlotte, married a Jew and decided to convert. She even changed her name to Hadassah. I think it's completely crazy."

"Charles told me," Michael said, taking a sip of his coffee. "that they may not blow-up the Dome of the Rock. It's possible that they will build the temple right next to the Muslim shrine."

"Do you believe him?"

Her question surprised him. It occurred to him that he'd never questioned Charles' truthfulness. "I believe him," he said. "There are many things that you could say about Charles Bishop; you could say that he is obsessed with Newton and the temple in Jerusalem, but I'm certain he is not a liar."

Rachel examined him through narrowed eyes, her lips pursed. "Building the temple right next to the Islamic structure is a recipe for disaster. I don't see how the Muslims could accept it, certainly not the extremists."

"Rachel," Michael said with a frustrated sigh, mulling over his next words carefully. "I have to be honest with you and, of course, with Stewart. At this point, I'm not so sure what my role is and what I'm doing here."

"Michael," she replied, "I'll bring this to Stewart; however, I have no question about your role."

"Enlighten me, please," he said to the young lady.

"You're an insider, Michael, our eyes on the ground, so to speak. You collect information on what might turn out to be a most volatile situation."

"I guess you're right," he said. "It's just that these people are so sincere, and they have such a wonderful community. I get confused."

"Don't let them get to you," she warned. "As I see it, you're doing a crucial job, and one day, we'll all have to thank you."

He took another sip of his coffee while pondering how much he wanted to share. "I had a one-on-one meeting," he finally said.

She curiously looked at him, both eyebrows raised, and prompted, "With?"

"Charles."

"Let me guess," she said, "you found him charming."

"Well, yes, but more than that."

"More than charming?"

"He truly cares about his people, and about … me."

"I hope you didn't tell him anything you weren't supposed to."

"I didn't, but he made me question … I mean, he's an incredible man. I never met anyone like him."

"Incredible man?" Rachel's tone was snappy, "so incredible that he's willing to drag humanity into an apocalypse? Michael, don't you see that he's getting into your head?"

"I'm just trying to make sense of it all," Michael said. "He's a loving person and highly intelligent. How could he be behind the horrendous plan that we ascribe to him?" Michael had a hard time accepting that Bishop would lie to him, but Rachel's words did make sense. He needed to keep his guard up.

"Obviously, there are two sides to him," Rachel said. "To understand him, all you need to do is look at a few prominent leaders throughout history and see that when a person is convinced of his absolute truth, he can become extremely dangerous and destructive. Look at Adolf Hitler, Josef Stalin, Mau Zedong, and Pol Pot: all of them murdered millions for the sake of their ideas. Then you have the religious fanatics, like the zealots of the Christian Inquisition, or an extremist like Osama Bin Laden—"

"I didn't realize how passionate you are about this operation," Michael interrupted, raising his hands defensively.

"I'm passionate about living my life in a sane world, and I majored in history." She smiled. "I know about men who think they know better than anybody. Michael, you expected

222

to find a bad guy who is dreadful and ugly, not a beautiful, charismatic person who is confined to a wheelchair, which naturally draws our empathy."

"Charles is compassionate," Michael said. "He loves his people, and they love him."

"His people!" Rachel said. "That's exactly what I'm talking about. You have to be one of *his people*; if you're not, then you might as well burn in hell." She finished her pie. "Delicious pecan pie, by the way."

"Tell me," Michael changed the subject. "Why does Stewart need the recordings of Bishop's discourses?"

"His wife, Irene, is a computer genius. She's working on an algorithm," Rachel said, her expression serious.

"An algorithm?" Michael smiled.

"Okay," she said, "I don't really know what an algorithm is. I majored in history, and I also took acting classes, so you can tell I'm not technologically oriented. I know that they want to create a large pool of Charles' words, but I'm not sure how they plan to use that pool."

"Sounds like Stewart has got some tricks up his sleeves," Michael said.

"He hired a guy to help with this project," Rachel said, "someone named John, though I'm quite sure that's not his real name. He's a skilled hacker, and he's quite strange."

"I heard about him," Michael said. "Stewart's collaborated with him several times over the years."

"Michael," Rachel took a deep breath, "I brought you something from Stewart."

"What is it?"

"You're not going to like it." She pulled a small, square package, wrapped in a brown paper from under her chair, pushed it in his direction, and cautioned, "don't open it here."

"I won't open it here if you tell me what's inside."

"It's an NVD." She smiled mischievously.

"What?"

"A night-vision device."

"And why on earth would I need it?" Michael balled his hands into fists.

"Stewart says that if you can find a chance when Bishop is away from his home in the evening, go in there and photograph whatever documents you may find."

"Just like that, huh?"

"There's also a small night-vision camera in the package."

224

"So, why doesn't Stewart go there at night and take pictures himself if he thinks it's so easy?"

"He doesn't think it's easy. He appreciates what you're doing, but he keeps saying that the stakes are high and—"

"Yeah, I know," Michael said. "We have to prevent a world war, but in the meantime, it's my ass that's on the line."

Rachel stared at him open-mouthed, as she'd never seen Michael that angry or heard him use vulgar language.

He shook his head and growled, "There's no way I'm breaking into Bishop's cabin. I've told Stewart many times that I'm not a spy."

"I know you did," she said softly. "So, only do what you can if the opportunity presents itself."

Reluctantly, Michael took the package and stuffed it into his backpack.

"You know, Rachel," Michael said, "I will go with the group to Jerusalem. I wonder how I'll communicate with Stewart from there."

"In the same way that you're communicating here," she said.

"Through you?"

"Yep, it will be my opportunity to visit my nutty sister."

Chapter 35

It was already dark when Michael made his way to the dining room, to have supper with the people he lived with and grew fond of during the past two months. It was a rainy evening, and the cold wind signaled the end of summer.

Near the dining room, Michael noticed Bishop's golf cart, indicating that Charles was joining his people for supper. It meant that everyone would be in the dining room, and that was Michael's opportunity—if he intended to act on McPherson's most recent request.

I am not a spy, Michael moaned to himself as he briskly walked back to his cabin to get the night vision equipment. Although McPherson had suggested that he invade Charles' personal quarters, Michael felt that such action went beyond spying. It would be an actual betrayal and a show of disrespect. Despite Michael's objection to Bishop's plan, he still held immense respect for him, so he opted for the computer center—where he'd never been.

He advanced quickly, staying in the forest's shadows and away from the few lampposts lighting the graveled path that led to the center. *I am not a spy*, he kept telling himself, having a particularly hard time since he wasn't sure the mission was essential. Located about a hundred yards from the dining hall, the computer center was one of the largest structures on *God's Land*. Surrounded by tall, forest trees, as if hiding in plain sight, the compound was dark once Michael got there. The high-tech staff, headed by Charles and David, usually worked long hours and into the night, so Michael assumed they might have just gone for supper, which narrowed his window of opportunity.

He knew that most of the buildings on the estate, private dwellings as well as public areas and workplaces, were not locked. Members of the community trusted each other, neighboring estates were far away, and no one was around to trespass from the outside.

If he were lucky, the computer center would not be locked. A lit porch served as the compound's main entrance. Michael's heart pounded as he looked around to make sure no one was there. He quickly strode to the entrance and pushed down on the door's handle, only to find that it was locked.

Now what? He wondered what to do as he withdrew into the darkness. *Maybe it's better this way. At least I could tell Stewart that I tried.* He walked around the building, fumbling in the dark. There was a small door at the rear. Michael pushed down the handle, and it opened. He hoped to find it locked so that he could abort the mission. He let out a resigned sigh.

I'm not a spy. Breathing rapidly, he entered the dark compound. He left the back door open and put on the night-vision goggles.

At first, he didn't see anything, which required him to pull out his cell phone and use it as a light source. He didn't need to turn on the flashlight app; just the device being turned on provided sufficient light and helped him maneuver in the darkness.

Once he got to the main operations area, he turned off the phone and slid it into his pocket. Although the lighting in the room was turned off, the many tiny lights shining from various computers and other digital equipment offered enough ambient illumination. His night-vision goggles amplified those minor lights, so he could see the room quite well.

Two computer workstations sat in the center of the room. Although he wasn't a computer expert, Michael recognized those machines as especially powerful supercomputers. He remembered seeing similar machines in the computer center of his university. Each workstation was connected to two large screens. One station was clearly Charles', as it had no chair, allowing Charles to roll in on his wheelchair. Michael guessed the other one to be David's. Other, simpler computers were connected to just one monitor each, so Michael assumed they were operated by support staff. On the wall behind David's two screens was a childish painting along with the writing, *Daddy I love you.*

Michael decided that trying to penetrate Charles' computer would be rude and disrespectful, so he sat on the other chair. He moved the mouse, and the two screens glowed as the machine came to life. A popup flashed onto the screen, demanding a password. What did he expect? A welcoming invitation? Michael tried 2520, only to get a *wrong password* message.

So, what could it be?

Since he couldn't easily break into the machine, he pulled out the night-vision camera that he received from Rachel and started to photograph the papers on the desk and in the drawers. Looking at his wristwatch, he noted that he'd been there for five minutes. It felt like an eternity. He got up and photographed some papers stapled to a large board when he saw a list of the group members and their dates of birth. He remembered seeing such lists in other offices where he was employed, so that people wouldn't forget to wish each other a happy birthday.

Going over the list, he found what he was looking for: David Richardson and his date of birth. Knowing that many people used their birthdates as their passwords, he went back to the computer, entered the date, and once again received a *wrong password* message. He tried inserting the date in reverse: first the year, next the month, then the day, and… *voilà!* He was inside.

Now what? Time was ticking. He looked through the computer's desktop, which was very organized. A file named *'Pass'* drew his attention; he figured it was short for *Passwords. This is the list I'm after.* Clicking on the file, he was prompted to enter another password. *Darn.*

He typed 2520. *Wrong Password.* David's birthdate, forward and backward? *Wrong Password.*

All of a sudden, he was stroked from behind. *What is it?* Whatever it was, moved next to him and touched his leg.

Michael's body went rigid as it became very clear he was not alone in the room!

He jumped to his feet, heart racing, and quickly scoured the space until he found the source of his panic: a curious black and white cat. *Jesus, kitty, you almost gave me a heart attack.*

Once again, his gaze was drawn to the childish drawing on the wall—a small blue house with a red roof, oversized people's heads that filled entire windows, and the writing: *Daddy I love you.* Michael examined it from up close and noticed that the child signed her name. He didn't perceive it when he first saw the drawing, but there it was: *Emily.*

Daddy I love you, Emily. He went back to the file titled *Pass* and when prompted for a password, he entered *Emily.*

"Wrong Password."

Perhaps backward? He typed *ylime.*

It opened, and there it was, a list of passwords. With the small camera, he photographed the many passwords displayed on the screen.

He needed to hurry and get out of there. While trying to restore everything to its original place, he heard the crunch of tires on gravel out front.

Michael hurried to the back door, exited the building, and gently closed the door behind him. He breathed a sigh of relief and, hiding in the shadows, felt protected by the darkness. Although it was cold outside, he was sweating.

He heard the front door open. Bright lights flooded the building's interior. Then, he listened as heavy boots pounded back and forth as if examining the place. After a short while, the sounds of the footsteps subsided, and the lights were turned off. From his hiding place, Michael heard Ruth's voice as she talked on the phone. "All clear," she said, "it was just a cat."

Michael headed back to his cabin. He darted from shadow to shadow, avoiding the lampposts and feeling like a wild, nocturnal animal. The swift operation required his full concentration, and he had no time to think of the consequences of getting caught. Was the gain worth the risk? Despite his apparent success, he wasn't sure.

He was filled with mixed emotions. On the one hand, he naturally felt relieved at fulfilling the mission. However, he had no sense of exhilaration or even contentment about his accomplishment.

Though he knew he shouldn't feel guilty, he still hated to find himself being untruthful with people who trusted and respected him. He'd come to *God's Land* thinking he would find a group of dangerous lunatics. Instead, he'd arrived at a nurturing community where he'd found people who believed their actions would contribute to the creation of a better world. Michael didn't share their way of thinking or their goals, but he saw that they genuinely believed they were serving a good cause and a higher purpose.

Chapter 36

Charles Bishop and his wife Mary were the only residents of *God's Land* who didn't regularly eat their meals in the dining room. Michael figured that Bishop's disability was the reason, not a need to maintain distance from his people. However, when Bishop and Mary did attend a meal, they had special seats reserved for them.

People were still eating and chatting when Michael walked into the dining room after hurriedly changing his sweat-soaked clothes. He thought he ought to appear as if he'd just gotten up from an afternoon nap, but wasn't sure how to do that. He served himself a small meal of steamed vegetables and ate it fast, understanding that Bishop was about to speak.

Indeed, within a short time, Bishop announced he wanted to say a few words. Conversations stopped and everyone curiously waited to hear their revered leader.

"People, friends," Bishop said, "in a couple of days, I'm sending most of you to Jerusalem. The time has arrived, all preparations have been completed, and the date has been set."

Michael's body tingled.

"Here, on the land," Bishop continued, "only a handful of people will remain to take care of the most necessary tasks. I believe that after our undertaking is successfully completed, most people will return right away. So, in about twelve days, this place will thrive again." He gazed out at his people and his smile widened, as if he sensed their growing excitement.

"Just for the record, I am staying here, although I would love to be with my people in Jerusalem at this auspicious time. With me, there will be a small staff that will include Mary, of course. From here, I'll control the operation in Jerusalem, and I've asked David to assist me at the helm.

"I have also asked Susan and Judy to stay and continue to take care of the kids. As far as any other tasks, I can assure you that if we can't manage all the affairs of the land, then we'll hire temporary help from Olympia. So, you have nothing to worry about. Does anyone have a question?"

Across the dining hall from Michael, Ron raised a hand.

"Yes, Ron." Charles nodded in his direction.

"So, when is the big day?" Ron asked.

"Next Wednesday!" Bishop exclaimed. "To stay aligned with the prophecy, it will start on the twenty-fifth day of the Jewish month of Cheshvan, which is the second month of the Jewish calendar year. We'll commence our operation at zero hour, which is midnight. So, we have *twenty-five* and then *two* and then *zero*, which is twenty-five twenty."

Bishop now looked in Michael's direction. "After our goal is achieved, I'm calling everyone to return here as soon as possible. The one person to remain in Jerusalem is Michael. He will be our representative and spokesperson over there. Michael will have to handle the all-important mission of explaining our objectives. He'll have to convince people all over the world that we want peace between the great religions. Over summer, you all had the opportunity to meet Michael. You've seen how diligent and charming he is, and you saw his courage and intelligence. Although he has been with us only a short time, I believe he's the right man for the job."

With everyone examining him and nodding favorably, Michael worried he was going to blush.

"Thank you, Bishop and everyone, for giving me this opportunity," Michael muttered.

"Mary," Bishop turned to his attentive wife sitting next to him, "please read aloud a short excerpt from the book of Zechariah in the Old Testament."

Mary nodded, opened her Bible to a marked location, and started to read:

"Therefore this is what the LORD says: 'I will return to Jerusalem with mercy, and there my house will be rebuilt. And the measuring line will be stretched out over Jerusalem, declares the LORD Almighty.'"

"Thank you, Mary." Charles smiled at her.

Michael enjoyed listening to her warm voice while looking at her beautiful and alluring face. He thought he could listen to her no matter what she read.

"It's important to look at our mission as a continuation of our spiritual work and prayers," Bishop said. "Praise be to God, and good night."

As people dispersed, one by one they passed by Charles who extended both his hands to shake theirs. While looking into their eyes, he blessed each of them and wished them a successful journey. When Michael passed by him, Bishop asked him to stay behind a little longer.

"Just an update for you, Michael," Bishop said after everyone exited. "We've scheduled a press conference at the King David Hotel on Thursday — one day after the auspicious day — at eleven o'clock in the morning. They're expecting you."

"The King David Hotel," Michael repeated with a nod.

"Have a safe journey," Bishop said, "and may God be with you always."

Chapter 37

The following day, Michael got a ride to Olympia with Ron to meet up with Rachel and deliver the recordings and the pictures he'd taken at the computer center.

"Could you tell me about Charles Bishop?" Michael asked Ron as the man rounded a sharp corner onto a section of the road lined with towering pines that blotted out the sun's glow. "I'd like to get a picture of the man, and any information might be useful when it is time to present our views to the world."

"Well, you came to the right place. Nobody knows Charles as well as I do." Ron said with a broad smile. After a pause, he added, "except for Mary, of course."

"So, you've known him for many years?"

"Yep, we come from the same town in Texas. I grew up in a poor neighborhood, and Charles was a rich boy, but we still became good friends. Charles never lorded it over me."

"You knew his family?" Michael asked.

"I've seen them," Ron answered. "But I wasn't allowed in their house. I didn't like the place anyway; it was too tidy for me. His father was a decorated Air Force pilot and his mother a snooty lady who was a senior partner in a large law firm.

"The Bishops had two kids," Ron continued, "Charles and his big sister, Angela. In my head I called her *Angel*, she was so pretty.

"Their folks held very high expectations for them, way higher than any reasonable folks, if you ask me. And they were never 'round. Always left the kids to nannies, you see…"

"So, you were not allowed to visit because you were poor?"

"Yep. I wasn't the type of person they wanted their kids to hang out with, you know; I was white trash. Charles' parents were also fervent Protestants who held contempt for other religions, primarily Catholics and Jews. The rules and discipline were rigid, and appearance was extremely important for the Bishops. Their house and cars were always spotless, and their kids were well-dressed and well-behaved. I knew Charles' parents told him not to play with me, but he disobeyed them on that one.

"They got hit real bad a couple of times, though. First time was when Angela got pregnant. She was just a teen and didn't know how to tell her folks, 'cause they were right set against abortion. She was real scared of bringin' shame to the family, so, she rode herself right into a cliff one night. Guess she hoped it'd look like an accident. And that's what their parents believed, 'cause no way they wanted to think she done committed suicide. The only one knew the facts was Charles."

"He never confronted his parents?"

"He probably didn't think it would do any good." Ron shrugged. "Second time they roughed it was when Charles got booted from the Air Force. He wanted to be like his old man, you see, and was trainin' to be a pilot."

Michael gaped at him.

Ron continued, "Charles was accused of robbin' a jewel store in one of 'em towns next to the base. His pops knew some mighty people and pulled a few strings to keep him from being court-martialed. The judge was an old friend of the family, so he bent a few rules."

"But," Michael interrupted, forehead crinkling, "if he was rich, why did he need to rob a jewelry store?"

"He didn't!" Ron exclaimed. "It was me. I was stationed at the same base, trainin' to become an aircraft mechanic. My pops was gonna die if I didn't get him the money for a procedure. I was right desperate."

"And you'd let him take the blame?"

"He made me! You see, he knew his folks would bail him out, but I would have gone to jail for a long, long time. And my pops would died."

"And Charles stayed in the army, right?"

"They made him leave the Air Force and all that as part of the agreement, but he went into the Marines and did mighty well, I might add. He shot through them ranks faster than none other and got promoted to lieutenant colonel. All of that ended when he got hurt in a battle. Nearly died."

"A remarkable man," Michael reflected.

"Remember, I told you," Ron said, "that there's nothin' I wouldn't do for him? If you went 'round and talked to people of our group, you'd find that quite a few folks have incredible stories to tell about him. Who knows, by now, you might have a story, too."

Michael nodded. "I do," he said, gazing out at the long stretch of winding, black road ahead of them. Tall pine and fir trees bordered their trail, interspersed with the occasional bulky willow. Michael noted Ron drove the SUV with only two fingers, but still managed to make the ride smooth and comfortable.

"And Mary?" Michael prompted.

242

"She's also quite amazing," Ron said. "You see, she and Charles were high school sweethearts. I know for a fact that most girls would've abandoned him after his injury, but not Mary. She pretty much sacrificed her life to take care of him. It's possible that without her, Charles wouldn't have survived his injury."

"Thank you, Ron," Michael said. "That's an incredible story. Do other people know? I mean, about the robbery?"

"It ain't a secret anymore," Ron replied, "though I rarely talk about it, and Charles is sure not gonna discuss it. You wanted to get a picture of the man, and I gave it to you."

***

Ron was quiet on the way back to *God's Land*.

"Did you get everything done?" Michael asked.

"Yep."

"Do you have everything you need for the trip to Jerusalem?"

"Yep."

Ron's eyes were fixed on the road ahead, but his jaw was tense. An anxious knot formed in Michael's stomach.

"Is there a problem?"

"Nope."

Ron's behavior was in sharp contrast to his willingness to chat and share information on the way to Olympia. His face was tight, his expression hard. Cold. Distant. He wouldn't meet Michael's gaze.

"Are you okay?"

"I'm fine."

Michael decided to leave him alone, assuming Ron regretted divulging information earlier.

They were nearing the halfway mark on the drive back and hadn't seen another car in upwards of half an hour when Ron guided the SUV to the side of the road, parked in front of a large grove of trees, and switched off the engine. He drew a pack of cigarettes from his pocket, pulled himself a cigarette, lit it, and turned to face Michael while taking a long drag.

"I didn't know you smoked," Michael said. He'd never seen anyone of Bishop's people smoke.

"I smoke when I'm upset," Ron said.

"What happened?" Michael asked, having an ominous feeling.

"I just broke up with my lady," Ron said with a shattered voice. "She was the love of my life."

"I'm sorry to hear that," Michael stared at Ron, trying not to gape. He knew Ron as a happily married man and a good father to his two kids. He often saw him in the dining room with his wife, where they were almost always touching each other and smiling or giggling.

"Charles expects us all to be faithful to our spouses. But what can ya do? Sometimes life happens. I figured if God didn't want me to fall in love, why'd he send Katie my way? But then I was thinkin'… if this was a test o' sorts, I failed hard. *Hard.* And ya know what's the worst part?"

"What?" Michael whispered. The usually stoic man's eyes shone with moisture.

"Worst part is I don't regret my relationship with Katie. That love was the most wonderful thing that ever happened to me. I mean, I didn't even know I could feel that way. She was the reason for my gettin' up in the morning, and I could sit with her forever and just talk and look into her beautiful eyes."

"So, why did you break up?" Michael asked gently.

"I didn't plan on endin' the relationship," Ron said. "But when we met today, I suddenly realized I couldn't go to Jerusalem to build the holy temple while living a lie. I felt I should come clean. I mean, I'm going to the holy land, to *God's Land*, to the Temple Mount, and I can't carry this burden of cheatin' with me. You see, Katie is also married and a Christian woman, and we're violating the seventh commandment: Thou shalt not commit adultery."

Michael examined Ron appreciatively.

"Now you know, Michael." Ron took a long drag on the cigarette, exhaled, and gazed into the distance for a moment before continuing. "I've been using my role as community driver to cheat on my wife." He finished his cigarette, lit another one, and muttered, "You're seeing someone too."

"What?" Michael felt as if his heart skipped a beat.

"I've seen you sitting in a café with an attractive blonde."

Michael felt dizzy. Had he been exposed? Did Ron know about his spying?

"We all have weaknesses," Ron said between puffs of tobacco. "I know your situation is different than mine. You're separated from your wife, so you could say you're not really cheatin', and though your secret is safe with me, I'd still advise you to be more secretive about your affairs."

"Thank you, Ron," Michael said, shaken. "I'll take your advice into consideration." He breathed a sigh of relief.

Back at his cabin, Michael sat on his couch and rubbed his face. *It had been prudent of McPherson to assign Rachel as my contact. If Ron had seen me talking to a man, he might have reached a very different conclusion.*

Chapter 38

Jerusalem 1967 AD

Twelve-year-old Uri was scared. The news on the radio wasn't encouraging. The chance of avoiding the looming war seemed to decrease with every militant statement by the leaders of the neighboring Arab countries. Uri was a curious Israeli child who followed current events by reading the newspapers and listening to the radio.

He grew up in a divided Jerusalem, where his countrymen, the Israelis, ruled the western neighborhoods, and the Jordanians were in control of the eastern sections, including the old city and the Temple Mount. In between the two sides was a border with fields of barbed wire fences and landmines. That was the only reality that Uri and his friends had ever known, and they didn't think it would ever change.

His parents were atheists. They didn't observe most of the Jewish religious practices. They didn't eat kosher foods and had no problem driving on Saturday—the so-called holy Sabbath. But Uri had friends who wore kippahs on their heads to signal their belief in God, and in the streets of Jerusalem, he often saw Orthodox Jews with their long beards and strange black outfits.

"Is there a God?" He posed the question to his parents when he was around six years old, as they sat around the dinner table.

His father, who immigrated to Israel from the United States, took a spoon of rice from his plate and dispersed it on the table. "If there is a God," he said, "let's see him pick-up the rice and hold it in the air."

Uri stared at the rice, which remained in its place.

"If there was a God," his mother said, "then your grandparents would be sitting here with us and would not have been killed in the Holocaust."

She always had tears in her eyes when she talked about the Holocaust, and about her loved ones who perished in the death camps. She was a little girl during World War II and the only member of her large family who survived. She owed her life to nuns who hid her in a Christian convent, where they raised her as a Christian. They even changed her name from Dina to Christina. As a little child, Uri could not comprehend the magnitude of the Holocaust, but he knew that something really, really bad had happened to his people.

When Uri was little, his parents promised him he wouldn't have to serve in the army when he grew up.

"By then, we'll have peace with our Arab neighbors," his dad assured him. "We'll be able to take a train to Damascus and eat Falafel over there."

"Our people are sensible and diplomatic. We will know how to avoid a war," his mother told him once—after he had run into his parents' bedroom, following a nightmare in which he had to fight in a horrible war. "You won't see the horrors of war, my love," his mother embraced him.

They no longer mentioned that possibility, because peace looked more and more like an unattainable vision. Now, three Arab countries—Egypt, Syria, and Jordan—were massing their armies around the borders of his small country. Their statements were clear and unmistakable: "We will conquer Palestine and throw the Jews to the Mediterranean Sea."

Uri was an intelligent child. He knew that the Arabs significantly outnumbered the Israelis when it came to soldiers, tanks, airplanes, and money to buy more weapons. So, naturally, he was scared.

250

When the leader of Egypt, Gamal Abdel Nasser, announced that he was closing the Straits of Tiran to Israeli vessels, Uri's father said in a somber tone of voice, "Now the war is unavoidable."

Shortly after that, he was called to his reserve army regiment, where he served as a tank commander in the southern, Egyptian, desert front.

On the morning of June 5, Uri heard a strange announcement on the radio: "Early this morning, the Egyptian forces started to move toward our border. Our forces went to block them, and a fierce battle erupted."

Uri knew that his country was engaged in a fierce war. He chose not to share his distresses with his mother who was dealing with fears of her own; mostly, she was petrified about her husband's fate.

The news on the radio, however, sounded encouraging: "Our forces are winning in all the fronts. They are moving deeper into the Egyptian controlled Sinai Peninsula, and gaining ground against the Jordanians in the West Bank."

But Uri also tuned into an Egyptian radio station that broadcasted in inarticulate Hebrew. The message was different: "This is Cairo Radio," said the announcer in an ominous voice, "our forces are moving toward Tel Aviv."

Uri and his friends chose to believe the Israeli version of the news and they enjoyed making fun and imitating the Egyptian broadcaster's heavy accent. However, lying in his bed before falling asleep, he experienced a moment of horror when he considered, only for a moment, the possibility that the Egyptian radio broadcaster was telling the truth.

Uri didn't need the radio to know that fierce battles raged in Jerusalem, as he heard the sounds of gunfire, explosions, and artillery bombardment that the Israelis and Jordanians fired at each other. He also saw Israeli aircraft attacking and bombing the Jordanian positions.

Israeli radio continued to report incredible victories, so incredible that the intelligent 12-year-old started to doubt those accounts.

"Most of the Sinai Desert is in our hands," announced an excited reporter, "and our forces are advancing toward the Suez Canal."

Uri could only think about his father, who was serving on that desert front. *God, please bring my father home unharmed.* For the first time in his life, Uri prayed.

252

On June 7, merely two days after the start of the war, young Uri, who hardly moved away from the radio, heard the most astounding announcement by a reporter who was overcome by emotions: "I am at the Kotel. I'm touching the stones of the Western Wall."

Throughout his life, Uri, like other Israeli children, had heard about the Western Wall, the only remnant of the original walls that surrounded the Temple Mount. For many years, getting to the wall was an unattainable dream for his people, because the Jordanians who controlled the site, viewed the Israelis as their arch enemies, and didn't allow such visits.

Could it really be in the hands of the Israeli soldiers? Could he visit that sacred place? Uri leapt from his bed and dashed into the kitchen, where his mother sat at the table, listening to a radio of her own. Their eyes met; his mother's glistened, and a tear rolled down her cheek as she gave him a soft smile.

A few hours later, a reporter interviewed an army colonel who proclaimed, "The Temple Mount is in our hands."

Uri no longer heard frightening explosions and bombardments. The silence of abandoned streets quickly transformed into the bustle of a thriving city.

After another two days of fighting, the radio announced that the Israeli army had conquered the Syrian Golan Heights. The war ended after a mere six days, with a decisive Israeli victory. The three Arab countries suffered a crushing and humiliating defeat.

Unharmed, Uri's father returned from the war. He downplayed his involvement, and said that the Air Force cleared the way for his tank brigade, and they didn't encounter much resistance. Uri thought he said so in order to calm his wife who had been sick with worry he was in harm's way.

Uri, along with his parents, visited the Arab sections of Jerusalem, which had always been on the other side of the impassable border. Like many of their countrymen, they felt triumphant, even euphoric, as they enjoyed discovering the colorful Arab market, which contained the *Via Dolorosa*— Jesus' last journey on earth. Uri looked at the Arab sellers in the market. Are they still the enemy? At that moment, they appeared more eager to sell their goods to their new, wealthier clients than to start another war.

The family continued to the Temple Mount, where they entered the Dome of the Rock and beheld the massive rock

254

inside. A guide explained that, on that very rock, '*the foundation stone*,' Abraham had intended to sacrifice his son, Isaac.

"So, Dad," Uri asked. "Are we going to rebuild the temple?"

"No!" his father answered. "The religious people are against it."

"The religious Jews?" Uri didn't understand.

"Yes," his father said. "They think that we have to wait for the Messiah to come. Some of them believe that he will come riding a donkey or some silly thing like that."

Chapter 39

Michael had dinner in the dining room for the last time. Tomorrow morning, he'd be on his way to Jerusalem.

After the meal, he went to his cabin and packed his belongings. He looked around the room fondly, recognizing how much he liked his cozy, wooden space, his bachelor's nest after years of marriage.

He realized how quickly he got used to the communal life and how much he loved the land and the people. He knew he would miss the shared meals and the atmosphere of solidarity. He would miss Charles, perhaps the most compassionate person he'd ever met. He would also miss Mary. Did she notice how much he liked watching her?

A feeling of loneliness descended on him. He called his home in New York, and his wife picked up the phone.

"Hi, Lanie." He forced as much cheerfulness as he could muster into his tone.

"Hi, Michael." She... didn't sound enthusiastic.

"I'm going to Jerusalem tomorrow."

"Good luck."

Michael waited a few seconds, but she didn't say anything else. No 'I'll miss you' or 'be careful.'

They both knew that they should be careful of what they say on the phone; after all, they were supposedly estranged. But were they still pretending? Didn't she sound truly distant? Upset at him? Had his mission created a real alienation between them?

"Can I talk to Linda?"

"She already went to sleep."

"Please kiss her good night for me and tell her that daddy loves her and will be home soon."

"I will, Michael. Take care of yourself."

"Goodnight, Lanie."

She hung up the phone.

He remained sitting with the phone in his hand for a few minutes. That wasn't the conversation he expected.

Melany sounded tired, weary. Michael didn't know what to make of it. He missed his wife and daughter, but he couldn't deny he was excited about the adventure ahead or that he cherished the past two months in *God's Land*.

Michael hoped that, when he returned, he'd manage to restore his connection with his wife, the love of his life. *I have to compensate her for the time I've been away. It's my obligation to explain why I had to go but now isn't the time. I must remain focused on the mission.*

He decided to clean the cabin. It wasn't late, and he wasn't tired. *I couldn't fall asleep anyway.* He swept the floor with a broom he'd found in the bathroom.

Then he opened his laptop and checked the weather and other news about Jerusalem. Nothing out of the ordinary over there. In the old city, a young Palestinian man stabbed and injured a middle-aged Orthodox Jew in an apparent terrorist attack. The injured man was rushed to a hospital. An angry Palestinian demonstration protested against archaeological excavations near the Temple Mount. The American embassy warned American tourists to be vigilant.

He found himself thinking about the writing on the wall. He remembered the cryptic message:

"MENE MENE, TEKEL, UPHARSIN."

Michael knew that the biblical prophet Daniel had already deciphered the message for the Babylonian King Belshazzar, about five hundred years before Christ. He also remembered that over the centuries, scholars and theologians continued to look for a secret meaning in the message, and some of them thought that it was composed of monetary numbers totaling 2,520. And yet, Michael sensed that if he only put his mind to it, he might find a whole new solution. But how could he even come close to solving the puzzle, considering he spoke neither Hebrew nor Aramaic? Perhaps in Jerusalem, he'd find a different angle that would help him unravel the mystery.

He thought about the prophet Daniel. The Babylonian king had offered him the third highest-ranking title in the kingdom, and showered him with fancy clothes and gold. But Daniel was not interested and told him to save his rewards for someone else.

Daniel knew he didn't belong in there. He was different, perhaps an outsider like me, and he remained loyal to his values. Michael's mother had once shared with him that initially, she'd planned to name him Daniel. Was that why he felt a kinship with the old biblical prophet?

It was getting cold, so Michael turned on the heater. Within minutes the cabin was pleasantly warm, and he could take off his long-sleeved shirt and remain in a t-shirt.

A knock sounded at the door. *It's 10:30 PM, who could that be?*

He opened the door.

Michael knew he should have been surprised, but he wasn't. Maybe subconsciously, he'd even been wishing for her companionship.

Despite the rain and wind, she stood before him wearing only a thin silk gown. Her hair was wet, and raindrops rolled down her bare, tan arms and legs. She looked up at him with ravenous eyes and said nothing.

He looked at her for a moment, hesitating.

"Can I come in?" she asked in her pleasant, deep voice.

"Mary, I don't think it's such a good idea."

"Why not?"

"We are both married and—"

"You are separated." She met his eyes, her blue gaze piercing. "Are you not?"

His thoughts went haywire. "And what about you?" He asked.

260

"Let me worry about my own affairs."

He felt torn. On the one hand, he wanted nothing more than to let her into the cabin; on the other hand, his moral compass warned him that such action could develop into something wrong. "What about Charles?" he asked.

"Charles knows that I'm not the Madonna. I am a woman, and sometimes I have a woman's needs."

He'd wondered about that, whether Charles in his disabled condition was able...

She shivered but continued to stand still, waiting for his invitation to enter. The rain plastered her hair to her head and the gown to her body, revealing dips and curves Michael had only imagined seeing until now. He couldn't help but notice the graceful slope of her shoulders and the shape of her legs. She looked wild as the raindrops whipped her head and shoulders and trickled down her unprotected body. Michael sensed how, as the rain hammered away the sacred intangibility he'd built up around her, so, too, were his defenses crumbling.

He could no longer keep her standing outside.

"Come in," he said in a hoarse voice.

She entered the warm cabin, and he closed the door behind her. As she passed him, he felt as if his body were magnetized, drawn toward her. He was awakened, way past the point of no return. He dimmed the cabin lights.

"Mary," he whispered as he peeled the soaked gown off her skin. He reached for a dry towel and dabbed her wet, naked body. Then he embraced her until she stopped shivering.

"Michael," she whispered back into his shoulder. Her voice sank into his skin.

He knew the only way he could quell the fire that burned through his entire being was to completely let go and merge with the beautiful woman who entered his cabin, asking him to love her.

Chapter 40

Melany

I had a bad day. Actually, it was a terrible day. This morning, I failed to protect a battered woman from losing custody of her kids.

Trisha is not without problems. Still, she loves her two little children more than anything in the world. However, her abusive husband is a rich and powerful man, and his lawyers managed to portray her as an unfit mother with a drinking problem. They also showed secretly taken photos of her allegedly having extramarital affairs.

I argued that her husband has a violent nature, and I managed to prove that the atmosphere in his house is that of intimidation, and not of nurturing, for the kids. Unfortunately, the male judge ruled against Trisha, even though the kids begged to stay with their mother. I don't think her husband really wants the kids; he just wants to hurt

Trisha, because she dared to leave him. I feel awful for failing to help her, so I decided to appeal the ruling, even though Trisha has no money to pay me.

Later in the day, I essentially broke up with Henry. I just wanted to be alone, but he convinced me to meet him at a fancy Italian restaurant. He started to ask me all kinds of weird questions about Michael and whether we're really separated. I told him I didn't want to talk about it. Afterward, in the car, he tried to kiss me. I shoved him away as hard as I could, got out of the car, and slammed the door. As I was leaving, he said he was sorry, and I said I hoped I'd never see him again, which is ridiculous since he's a partner in my law firm.

Before I went to bed, Michael called to tell me he was going to Jerusalem. He sounded lonely and needed reassurance, but I was too upset to offer any.

I think that by pretending to be estranged, we've actually grown apart from one another. I needed some encouragement myself. I wanted to tell him about those times when I thought someone was spying on me, and about noticing that the computer's camera was turned on without my doing it. But

264

then, I realized that he's got enough on his plate with the cult and going to Jerusalem and all that madness, so I just hung up the phone.

It dawned on me that Michael is still looking for a father figure to compensate for the lack of such authority when he grew up. It's sad because I know his adoptive father really loved him. So, now he's got two strong men who might fit the profile, two leaders who oppose each other. One of them is Stewart McPherson whom Michael adores. The other one is the cult leader. It's not something that Michael told me directly, but I sensed it from the way he talked about him in our phone calls. Now, he's on his way to Jerusalem. I know he believes he must prevent a horrible war, but maybe he's trying to please those two figures—to prove himself worthy of their acceptance and appreciation?

I want to hold him and tell him I love him as he is. He doesn't have to prove to me that he's worthy—I know he is. I want to tell him that he's a wonderful husband and a great father to Linda. I think that in going to Jerusalem, Michael is getting to the most dangerous part of his mission, and it scares me. I'm terrified that he'll martyr himself, sacrifice his life for what he believes in. I pray that he won't get carried away and that he'll remember he has a wife and a daughter who truly love him and wait for him to come home.

Chapter 41

"The world was not created until God took a stone called Even haShetiya and threw it into the depths where it was fixed from above till below, and from it the world expanded. It is the centre point of the world and on this spot stood the Holy of Holies."

- ***The Zohar***

Jerusalem, Present Day

Michael traveled to Jerusalem, along with several group members. Their flight landed in Ben Gurion Airport, near Tel Aviv, where they continued to Jerusalem by train.

Masquerading as Christian pilgrims, the group rented the whole floor of a hotel in the western part of Jerusalem. Michael learned that they also rented a large, bankrupted factory near the city of Modi'in on the outskirts of Jerusalem. In Modi'in, they constructed the sections of the temple—to be assembled on the Temple Mount. Most of the group worked around the clock, ate, and slept at the Modi'in site; still, every once in a while, they allowed themselves short vacations, when they stayed at the hotel in Jerusalem. During those vacations, they toured the city, especially the Temple Mount and its vicinity, to become familiar with the area.

The leader of the operation was introduced to Michael by his first name only, Paul. Michael recalled that, when he'd lurked on the group's web site, there was a person that called himself *Saint Paulus*, who was an explosives expert. Now, Michael suspected it was the same man.

Paul was Charles' right-hand man who has been with him for many years. While Charles was the spiritual leader of the group, Paul was the logistics manager. Michael heard that Paul was a former Air Force captain and helicopter pilot, and he had connections with several higher-ups within the Israeli armed forces. He ran the whole operation like a military campaign, requiring the group members to follow rigid standards of discipline and long hours of hard work.

Charles knew he could count on Paul's ability to get things done; and, indeed, thanks to Paul's tireless efforts, the plan was in place and ready to execute on the "auspicious day."

268

"I'd like to go to Modi'in and help with the preparations," Michael, who arrived in Jerusalem just two days before the so-called "auspicious day," told Paul.

At around forty years of age, Paul looked similar to most of the men in the group, sporting long hair and a beard.

He appeared energetic and busy—like he had no time to waste.

"Your job is to stay out of the way," Paul replied without prevarication. His phone rang, and he reached for it.

"Hi," Paul said in a business-like manner. "I've been waiting for your call. Let me just find a quiet place to talk." Paul walked away, leaving Michael wondering if that concluded their conversation. Michael was offended by how swiftly his offer of help was brushed off, and he hoped they did not learn any new damaging information about him.

Seconds later, Paul walked back through the door. "Listen, Mike," Paul locked Michael's gaze with his.

"My name is Michael," Michael corrected him.

"Whatever," Paul said. "I heard that you are a college professor who's going to be our spokesman."

"That's the plan," Michael confirmed.

"You must know," Paul continued, "That Charles is the most compassionate person I ever met."

"He is incredible," Michael nodded.

"I'm *not* a compassionate person," Paul stated. "Or perhaps I have a different perspective of what compassion is. The truth is, I was against bringing you onboard at such a late and delicate stage of the operation. As far as I'm concerned, the whole thing looks awfully suspicious."

"What do you want me to say?" Michael lifted his shoulders.

"Nothing," Paul said. "Just know that we are watching you, and you better not cross us!"

"I heard you," Michael focused on keeping his expression calm though his heart pounded hard. "Is that all?"

"For now," Paul said. His phone rang again.

Paul briskly walked away, and Michael watched him with mixed feelings: He didn't appreciate the way he'd been treated, but he couldn't be mad at the man for his astute assessment.

I should be careful around him, Michael told himself, noticing that he was sweating.

Michael chose to look on the bright side of Paul's refusal to accept his assistance. Now, he had two days to explore

Jerusalem, one of the most coveted cities in the world—by peoples and religions, as well as tourists.

Heading to the old city, he took the Jerusalem Light Rail, which was crowded with orthodox Jewish women and their many children.

Upon exiting the train, Michael found himself standing in front of the centuries-old wall, which still surrounded the ancient part of Jerusalem. Along with many tourists, he crossed the massive brick wall through the wide *Damascus Gate*.

Michael enjoyed exploring the lively and colorful Arab bazaar and marketplace, containing exotic sights, smells, and sounds he'd never encountered before. He bought an embroidered robe for Melany and a little oud—an Arab string instrument—for Linda, who'd started to show a musical inclination.

The market had narrow, cobblestone streets and was full of curious tourists from all over the world. Vendors actively approached the tourists, eager to sell their goods. Michael noted how, amid all the commotion, it was easy to forget that this city was desired by different and opposing nations and faiths. For a moment, one could overlook the wars and tremendous bloodshed that claimed the lives of thousands of civilians and soldiers through more than three thousand years. At a few strategic locations, Israeli soldiers were a reminder of the still tense situation. Armed with sophisticated assault weapons, they stood aside and attentively watched the crowds and the activity, ready to intervene in the event of a disturbance.

Michael walked the part of the market known as the *Via Dolorosa*, or "The Way of Grief." He tried to imagine Jesus, the skin of His back and legs ripped to shreds, His face bleeding from the thorns, lugging a massive cross on His back. He tried to imagine the weight, both physical and emotional, of being forced to carry the mechanism of one's own execution. Michael wasn't sure it was something that could be understood if one hadn't experienced it himself.

The *Via Dolorosa* ended at the Church of the *Holy Sepulcher*, believed to be where Jesus had been crucified. Michael entered the church but exited shortly afterward, as the place was crowded with pilgrims and tourists and looked overly commercialized.

***

The following day was the eve of the "auspicious day," the date Charles Bishop designated for executing his mission. At midnight the new, third temple would be formed, descending from the sky by helicopters in a complex operation. Being barred from helping in the preparations, Michael rose early and went to visit the Temple Mount, which had strict and limited visiting hours. *This is the place*, he thought while stepping onto the site. *This is what so many people have yearned for, fought, and died for, in ferocious wars. The Jebusites and the Hebrews, the Assyrians and the Babylonians, the Romans and the Greeks. In the end, the Muslims got the upper hand when led by Saladin, they defeated the Crusaders and ruled the place for centuries. And now? Will Charles Bishop and his devoted group write the next chapter?*

The possible repercussions deeply worried Michael. *Well, at least they're not planning to blow up the Dome of the Rock*, he thought, *but to build the temple next to it. Then it will be my role to convince the world—and mainly the Muslims—that we came in peace. Can I do it?* He wasn't sure. He took a deep, steadying breath.

He knew he had to preside over a press conference, already summoned for the following day, at the King David Hotel, and declare that he represented the group. Was this task too big for him? Or for anybody? Charles was right when he said that Michael was articulate, but Michael knew that he lacked experience. Could he deal with the tough questions that reporters were likely to ask? Such as why his leader presumed to decide the time of the temple's creation.

Michael chewed his lip as he considered all his options. There was still some time... should he go to the Israeli authorities and reveal the plan? There was no guarantee they would believe him. And what if they didn't take action in time? What if they arrest him?

A disturbing thought struck Michael: it dawned on him that somewhere deep inside of him, he wanted Bishop's plan to succeed.

He'd spent two months on *God's Land*, being part of a closely-knit community, working shoulder to shoulder with members of the group. Had Bishop's teachings found fertile soil in his inner core? Perhaps he'd become enamored with Bishop and his people, not to mention Mary? And maybe Mary came over that night for that specific purpose—to win him over and make sure he wouldn't turn against the group on that crucial hour? He immediately ruled out that possibility. Still, after all the hard work, didn't he want to see the exquisite building manifests overnight on the Temple

Mount? Where it belongs? Where it reigned more than a thousand years?

The Temple Mount was surprisingly serene in that morning hour. There were no signs of possible disturbances, like riots and clashes between fervent Muslim believers and the Israeli armed forces. Only a few tourists walked around and took pictures. A group of Italian pilgrims and their pastor entered the site. The pastor spoke Italian into a cordless microphone while his congregation, Michael assumed, listened to him via the identical pair of headphones they each wore. They crossed what was once the temple's courtyard and rounded a corner, walking out of sight. Michael wondered if they felt even a shred of remorse for the actions and cruelty of their ancestors. He doubted it. After all, they could claim that the Romans were hedonistic savages while they were modern realized Christians.

The Dome of the Rock turned out to be a magnificent structure. It was beautifully ornamented with intricate patterns and verses from the Muslim's holy book, the Quran. Its roof was the famous golden dome.

Michael stepped over to the entrance, where a few Arab men sat leisurely on old wooden chairs and smoked tobacco from a narghile.

"Can I go inside?" he asked.

"No!" said one of the men.

They examined him. Their eyes narrowed in a hostile and suspicious manner.

"Only Muslims!" said another.

Michael glanced inside through the open doors. He saw a section of a gigantic brown rock that looked massive. It had a height of about one yard, a width of two or three yards, and since Michael's view was obstructed, he couldn't tell how long it was.

So, this is the famous rock? He thought while walking away. *The foundation rock? The drinking stone? The navel point of the world? The spiritual junction of Heaven and Earth?*

Michael had his doubts. He'd read that the ancient Jebusites might have conducted the human sacrifice of young boys on that rock.

A cluster of armed Israeli soldiers, men and women, huddled not far from the Dome of the Rock, smoking cigarettes and seeming to enjoy the morning sunshine.

Various other structures were located on the Temple Mount. With the help of a tourist map, Michael recognized the bulky Al-Aqsa Mosque, which didn't trigger his interest. He searched for the structure that Bishop mentioned on his first day in *God's Land*, and there it was—the Dome of the Spirits or Dome of the Tablets. It was an octagonal cupola, located about 200 yards from the Dome of the Rock. Michael was surprised to find that it was only a few yards in diameter. After his conversation with Bishop, Michael further explored the subject. He'd discovered that, indeed, several notable researchers believed, like Bishop, that the Dome of the Rock was not situated where the temple used to be—and the Dome of the Spirits was a leading alternative for the right location.

Michael stepped inside the Dome of the Spirits, which was an open structure. Was it allowed? Oddly, no one was around to bar his entrance.

There was an ancient presence in that place, and invisible threads connected Michael to something intangible. He felt, somehow, that the world suddenly made more sense. A stillness settled over him, and for a moment, he let go of his anxieties, and just… *was*.

Was he standing on sacred ground? Near where the Holy of Holies stood two thousand years ago?

He examined the floor of the structure. In his research, he learned that the entire Temple Mount was paved, except those few square yards of the Dome of the Spirits, where the floor consisted of the original rock of Mount Moriah. Michael kneeled, laid his palms on the rock, and closed his eyes. Was he touching the foundation stone? The rock was warm to the touch as it absorbed the morning sun's rays.

A burst of frigid wind lashed his face, piercing through his jacket and setting his teeth chattering. Startled, he sensed that he'd stepped onto a forbidden ground for which he lacked authority... not the authority of man, but of a higher power.

He opened his eyes, rose, and looked around. Nothing has changed, not physically. But the sky suddenly seemed to press down on him, growing dark and warning that he was not supposed to be there.

"*Behold!*"

He heard a voice and felt his heart pounding. Frightened, he rushed out of the Dome of the Spirits.

What has just happened? Michael felt bewildered. *Where did the voice come from?*

Behold! I heard, but what does it mean?

Did it come from an old memory stored deep inside me? Or from an outside source? Maybe it came from the foundation rock? Or perhaps ... that inner part of me links to the foundation rock? And the foundation rock is the hub that is connected to everything in the world?

Michael looked around. There was certainly plenty of space for Bishop's temple, without intruding on the Dome of the Rock. But would the Muslims accept it? Agree to live side by side? In peace?

In his preparations for the journey, Michael read about the Islamic religion. He learned that the literal meaning of the word "Islam" was *submission*, and it was derived from the word *salam* which means *peace*.

He could use that in his press conference when he appealed to the Muslims to accept their new neighbor and live in peace and harmony. It would make a sensible argument. But upon further thought, Michael didn't believe the Muslims would agree to the existence of the new temple as a peaceful neighbor to the Dome of the Rock. Perhaps the moderate Muslims would consider the benefits of such coexistence, but their voice would not be heard among a chorus of furious extremists.

All in all, Michael thought, the Muslims' general attitude is likely to view the temple as a threat, with the potential of shaking the foundation of their religion. They would probably start rioting right away, and calls for a holy war would follow soon after, just as McPherson feared.

Chapter 42

The Temple of Solomon being destroyed by the Babylonians, it may not be amiss here to give a description of that edifice.

This Temple looked eastward, and stood in a square area, called the Separate Place: and before it stood the Altar, in the center of another square area, called the Inner Court, or Court of the Priests: and these two square areas, being parted only by a marble rail, made an area 200 cubits long from west to east, and 100 cubits broad: this area was compassed on the west with a wall, and on the other three sides with a pavement fifty cubits broad, upon which stood the buildings for the Priests.

- **Isaac Newton, The Chronology of Ancient Kingdoms Amended.**

Visiting hours ended, and non-Muslims were urged to vacate the Temple Mount. Michael took a selfie, standing next to the Dome of the Spirits, with the Dome of the Rock behind him.

After all, he was also a tourist, and he wanted to share his experiences with Melany and Linda.

After leaving the Temple Mount, Michael wanted to visit the Western Wall, which the Jews referred to as the Kotel. The place is sacred to the Jews, who believe it is the only remaining wall of the original Temple Mount, where both of their temples had once stood.

The square in front of the Kotel was crowded with mostly Orthodox Jews, garbed in black, who came to pray and touch the big rocks. Some of them followed the old practice of writing a message, or a plea to God, and inserting it in the crevices between the rocks. Michael watched an old man trying to push his special letter into a narrow crack. Unfortunately for the man, there were so many notes hard-pressed in the cracks that no room was left for his message. Every time he attempted to shove his paper in, it immediately fell out. Michael wondered what went through the religious man's mind. Was God refusing his message?

A line of soldiers waited to be sworn by their commanders to defend their country. Michael remembered Ruth, formerly an Israeli soldier, telling him that the Kotel wasn't the real thing. He figured that by now, Ruth was in Modi'in, helping her friends put the last touches on the new temple.

It was after 3:00 PM, definitely time to find something to eat, as Michael hadn't eaten anything since the sandwich he had for breakfast.

He tried to call Rachel, thinking that maybe they could eat together, but there was no answer.

Not far from the Western Wall's square, he saw stairs climbing a steep incline. He knew that was the direction of the old city where he could find various restaurants. He started to climb up the stairs, where on every curve, beggars pleaded for money. Although he didn't understand their language, Michael knew they all had stories of their dire circumstances and reasons why he should help them.

Eyes leaden and stomach aching, Michael didn't stop for the panhandlers until he reached the top of the stairs, where he took a moment to rest and gather his breath. Then he pulled a coin from his wallet and threw it into the collection box of an old beggar who played a jaunty tune on his clarinet.

He found himself in the Jewish quarter of the old city. Looking around, he saw plenty of restaurants and food stands one next to the other, and tables and chairs cluttered the sidewalk in front of them. A shish kebab restaurant drew his attention for a moment. Then the glowing sign on the neighboring shop read 'Holy Bagels' in purple letters. Michael went for the latter, perhaps because he needed a taste of home. In Brooklyn, he frequented bagel shops where he liked to order a toasted bagel with Philadelphia cream cheese.

He ordered a large bagel with smoked salmon, cream cheese, and lots of vegetables, heated on a hot plate. The serving was generous and delicious, and Michael took his time, enjoying his meal. He observed the people sitting nearby. None of them could suspect that, just before midnight, the whole city and the entire country would be affected by a blackout. At that time, their phones would not work, and, probably, the electricity to their houses would be cut off. Would they be asleep at that time, unaware that, when they awoke, they'd be in for an incredible surprise? Some of them might see the temple as a dream come true, while others might recognize it as the beginning of a nightmare.

At around 4:00 PM, his phone rang. Michael glanced at the device and didn't recognize the number. For some reason, he had an ominous feeling about the call.

"Hello?" he said, hoping it was Rachel.

"Hi, Michael."

Michael tensed. He recognized the voice of Stewart McPherson, and by the journalist's somber tone, Michael guessed there was a reason for the unexpected call, and it wasn't good.

"Stewart," Michael said. "I thought you'd connect with me only through Rachel."

"There's no time," McPherson said in a crisp tone. "Michael, this is an emergency, and we have no time for chit-chat. We managed to hack into the group's server. They're on to you, which is why they didn't inform you of their changed plan."

"Changed plan?" Michael almost dropped the phone.

"Michael!" McPherson said. "I'm talking on a scrambled line, but it's only minutes before they block the signal, so listen up! We deciphered most of their codes, and we hacked into their central system. They've known about your spying for some time—at least the people at the top. For some reason, Bishop chose to keep you in and not share the information with the rank and file. This explains why you weren't notified about the changes to their plan."

"What changes?" Michael demanded, suddenly feeling queasy.

"They're going to blow up the Dome of the Rock."

A ringing silence followed for a few long seconds. "Holy moly," Michael muttered, rubbing the inner corners of his eyes.

"Michael," McPherson said, "you must stop them, or there will be a horrible war."

"You think I don't understand that?" Michael flexed his fingers, "and where the hell is Rachel?"

Chapter 43

"The hour and the day no man knoweth, neither the angels in heaven, nor shall they know until he comes."

- **Doctrine and Covenants 49:7**

"Stewart," Michael tried to steady his voice, as the world around him became more and more overwhelming. "I have no idea how to go about stopping them."

"Do you know how to get to the Western Wall?" McPherson asked.

"Yes," Michael said, "in fact, I was just there."

"Go back to the Kotel," McPherson said. "Right next to it, there's a popular tourist attraction called the *Western Wall Tunnels*. These are tunnels that extend under the old city and explore long sections of Jerusalem during the time of the second temple.

"Have you been there?" Michael was curious.

"Five years ago," McPherson said. "Anyway, the operators of the site are most likely in cahoots with Bishop's group."

"Do the tunnels extend under the Temple Mount?" Michael asked.

"No," McPherson said, "at least not until recently. You see, the Israelis who conducted the excavation were cautious not to dig under the Temple Mount, fearing it would infuriate Muslims all over the world."

"I see," Michael said. "So, Bishop's people are doing what the Israelis wouldn't do; but, how can they work there if it's a popular tourist site?"

"Obviously," McPherson said, "they can't work during visiting hours, so they've been working at nights. By now, they must be pretty close to the Dome of the Rock. From going over their correspondence, I conclude that they need just a few more yards to be directly under the Muslim shrine. Then, they'll detonate a massive explosion that will bring it down."

"I'd assume they have a heavy-duty drilling machine," Michael said. "Working with hoes and pickaxes would take forever."

"You're right," McPherson said. "Also, they've managed to get a bunch of explosives in there, so someone within the Israeli security forces must be turning a blind eye."

288

"Or taking an active role in helping them," Michael said.

"Go there as a tourist," McPherson said, "and find a place to hide until the staff leaves for the day. The action will probably commence after closing time. Get a flashlight so that you won't drain your phone's battery."

"I have a flashlight," Michael said. "But even if I find them, how do I stop them?"

No answer.

"Stewart?"

The line went dead.

I told him I'm not a spy. Michael noticed that his palms were sweating.

Chapter 44

"But you, Belshazzar, his son, have not humbled yourself, though you knew all this. Instead, you have set yourself up against the Lord of heaven. You had the goblets from his temple brought to you, and you and your nobles, your wives and your concubines drank wine from them. You praised the gods of silver and gold, of bronze, iron, wood and stone, which cannot see or hear or understand. But you did not honor the God who holds in his hand your life and all your ways. Therefore he sent the hand that wrote the inscription.
"This is the inscription that was written:
"MENE, MENE, TEKEL, UPHARSIN."

- ***Book of Daniel, Chapter 5***

The site of the *Western Wall Tunnels* was located on the northern side of the Western Wall's square. Michael arrived in the evening and purchased a ticket for the last touring group, giving him two hours to fill. Seeing a sign advertising a virtual

290

reality tour of ancient Jerusalem, he opted to check it out. *It would be better to keep my mind busy, rather than worry about the mission.*

The VR tour was fascinating. Wearing a special helmet, he could look all around him. It was like actually being in Jerusalem two thousand years ago. He saw and heard people going about their trades, all clothed according to the ancient era. The central point of the tour was, of course, the temple. Once again, Michael saw the magnificent structure, the second temple, the one that stood in the time of King Herod, the time of Jesus. More than other visitors, Michael was familiar with the structure. On Bishop's estate, *God's Land*, he had already visited a temple that looked almost identical.

Exiting the VR presentation, he walked back to the Western Wall's square. It was getting dark, though the Kotel and the square were well lit with powerful floodlights. Michael knew that it snowed during winter in Jerusalem, but for an early autumn evening, his jacket was sufficient.

Once more, he tried to call Rachel. This time she answered, and Michael heard her voice carried over the hollers and screams of children.

"Michael," she tried to talk over their noise, "I'm with my nieces and nephews; they're driving me crazy; I have to babysit them until my sister gets back; what do you need?"

"Can you find a quiet place?" Michael yelled to overcome the kids' screams. Michael ground his teeth, trying to be patient. Didn't she understand he was at a crucial stage of the mission?

"Okay, I'm with you," she said. And, indeed, the kid's screams sounded muted. "I had to go to the bathroom to escape them."

"Rachel, this is no time for games. I need your help. They're on to me, and I can't do it all by myself."

"You're right, Michael," she said. "I'm sorry. I got carried away with—"

"Rachel?"

The line went dead.

Michael had one hour until his scheduled tour of the Western Wall tunnels and whatever arose afterward. He watched the many people who still gathered at the famous site. He couldn't help but feel wholly alone.

***

Looking at the Western Wall, made Michael reflect on another wall—*the Writing on the Wall* from the Book of Daniel. He remembered the inscription:

"MENE MENE, TEKEL, UPHARSIN."

He knew that, over the ages, many scholars had tried to decipher the meaning of the cryptic message. One of them was Isaac Newton.

The writing on the wall. Well, this was *the* wall, probably the most famous of all walls. Michael examined it as keenly as he could. Did it convey any message? Perhaps a different interpretation than the one given in the Book of Daniel? A message for *our* time?

There were enormous, chiseled rocks at the bottom. Michael remembered reading that some of the large rocks could weigh hundreds of tons. On top of the bottom layer were two layers of giant, chiseled rocks, smaller than the first layer. Michael wondered how the ancient Hebrews carried and lifted them into place.

As he looked higher and higher up the Western Wall, the size of the rocks decreased. At the top layers, the rocks were quite small, just regular building bricks. Bits of moss grew in several places, rooted in the slits between the rocks.

What did it all mean? What was the message? Was there a message? Michael's entire body tingled as though he were on the verge of cracking a secret. What was *God* telling him?

The different layers represented different eras in the history of the wall, the history of the Temple Mount, the history of Jerusalem. What separated those eras? *Think, Michael, think.* He concentrated.

And then it hit him.

Wars!

That was the story of the wall. Each era, defined by layers of rocks, began and ended with a war: holy wars, religious wars, crusades, jihad, military campaigns for domination, cruel bloodshed.

Michael's mind spun.

That was the message. The Writing on the Western Wall was telling him a story of wars. And now, on the verge of a new war, a total and colossal war, he had a chance to prevent it before it started. He *must* do anything within his power to stop it. So much suffering this war could bring to humanity, and for what? For religious fanaticism?

294

He needed to stop the wall from gathering more layers of smaller and smaller rocks until they became stones, gravel, and then pebbles, ashes, dust. Wars would eventually turn everything to dust. Michael kneeled on the hard-stone tile of the Western Wall's square and found himself praying for the first time in his life. *God, please give me the strength to stop it before it erupts.*

He remained kneeling with his eyes closed for several minutes. Had God heard him? He couldn't tell.

The paving-stone was cool to the touch, as it lost its heat soon after sunset. Just this morning, he had knelt and touched another floor, the bedrock of Mount Moriah, in the Dome of the Spirits on the Temple Mount; and the day was far from over.

Standing up, he sent one more gaze toward the Western Wall. There was another thing, another message … and then he remembered: Sir Isaac Newton. Three hundred years earlier, Newton stated that humanity's religions were once pure and had become corrupted over the ages. That picture was evident on the wall, with its beautiful chiseled rocks at the bottom, and the plain bricks on top.

"This is the wall of our holy mountain," an old Jewish beggar said, shaking Michael from his thoughts.

"Excuse me?" It was hard to understand the man's broken English.

"You are from America, right?"

"Yes, I am." Michael took a subtle step away from the man.

"It is called Mount Moriah, where the binding of Isaac took place according to the book of Genesis." The bearded man hunched over a walking stick, draped in a black derby. "The Temple Mount is where the holy temple once stood," the man continued with his pointless explanations, "and with God's help, it will be restored." His voice was hoarse, but his eyes sparkled as he spoke about the temple. He extended his cup toward Michael, pleading for money. "Are you Jewish?"

"No, I'm not," Michael said. He reached for his wallet, pulled a coin worth ten shekels, and dropped it into the man's cup.

"God bless you," the old man said and preceded to toddle on his way.

"Excuse me," Michael called to the man.

"What do you want?"

"What does the word *mene* means in Hebrew?" Michael followed a sudden hunch, uttering the first word of the Writing on the Wall.

"*Mene?*" Puzzled, the old man scratched his chin. "I'm not sure, perhaps you mean *mena?*"

"Yes, *mena,* what does it mean?" Michael said, huffing out a sigh.

"It means *prevent,* my son, *pre-vent.* Is there anything that you need to prevent?"

"Yes," Michael said. "I have to prevent a horrible war."

Chapter 45

Michael entered the site of the Western Wall Tunnels, where he joined a group of about ten people who signed up for a tour with an English-speaking guide. The tour might have been interesting, even fascinating, except that Michael was preoccupied with the challenging task ahead. He assumed it would require him to be at his best and improvise according to the conditions confronting him. While the guide explained how the Western Wall's massive rocks were transported and put into place, Michael looked for a place to hide when the tour concluded. He also looked for signs of new diggings, but didn't see any.

The excavation project was enormous. The small group progressed along a narrow trail that bordered on both sides by brick walls. The tunnel was artificially lit, but still, it was quite dark. In several places, the trail widened into prayer coves and even a spacious synagogue, where Orthodox Jews prayed silently while facing the massive rocks. One section was reserved for women. Michael noted how deeply the men and women were immersed in their prayers. It occurred to him that if they were praying for the resurrection of the temple, their plea would be answered much faster than they imagined.

The guide was a religious Israeli man wearing a crocheted kippah on his head, who talked with an American accent. While walking, he explained the history of the Temple Mount in the different eras.

"Excuse me," Michael asked the guide, "do these tunnels extend under the Temple Mount?"

"Absolutely not!" the guide answered. "However, I believe that digging under the Temple Mount would reveal treasures that surpass any archaeological project in the history of the world. Who knows, the Ark of the Covenant might be buried down there. Unfortunately, we can't explore that ground due to political sensitivities."

Michael examined the guide's expression as he thanked him. If he knew anything about a new excavation underway, he did a good job of concealing it.

After the tour, the group headed for the exit where they dispersed, going their separate ways. Michael remained at the site, which was about to close for the day. He pretended to examine some exhibited archaeological artifacts and read the information about them while searching for a place to hide. He spotted a tiny room, perhaps a large closet, not far from the lavatories. Since most of the tourists and service personnel had already left, Michael threw one last hasty glance around to make sure nobody watched him and slipped into the room, closing the door behind him. There was a small shutter in the door through which a tiny ray of light filtered through. Groping in the dark, he realized the room must have served the cleaning crew, as it contained brooms, buckets, and the like. His breathing was shallow as he sat on the ground of the dark and damp space, trying to relax. He thought of muting his phone but found he didn't have to, as there was no signal in the underground location.

What in the world am I doing? Have I gone crazy, hiding underground in such a foreign place? If the authorities catch me, they'll put me on the first plane to the U.S. or send me to a mental institution. What will I tell them? That I came to save the world?

Alone underground, darkness and shadows surrounded Michael. Gloom overcame him as he settled in for the long wait. He tried to envision images of Melany and Linda to brighten his lonely heart. He visualized coming home, and Linda joyfully running to embrace him.

300

He recalled a conversation with Melany, just a couple of days before McPherson called with information about the cult. The two of them had sat in the kitchen, drinking tea.

"Lanie," he'd asked, "are you happy with the way things are between us? I mean, have we started to take each other for granted?"

For a split second, she froze. He wasn't sure, but she might have even stopped breathing. He knew his question had hit home with her, and he started to regret bringing it up. Then she took a deep breath and looked directly at him.

"Hun," she answered, "we are in the valley."

"The valley?"

"Yes." She nodded. "That's life; there are peaks, and there are valleys. You can't expect to always be at the peaks. Life doesn't work that way."

He understood, accepted her elucidation.

"Tell me," he'd said, "how did you get so smart?"

She smiled, and her smile brightened his world, shining all the way from their kitchen in New York to the underground tunnel in Jerusalem.

Sitting in the tiny room, he reflected upon that conversation.

Was the valley not good enough for me? Is that why I went away? Am I better off now? Is this the peak I was looking for? Hiding in this damp and moldy closet?

It dawned on him that he was in some kind of a confession booth. The small room and the shutter … There was no priest around to listen to him, though perhaps being so close to where the Holy of Holies used to be, one did not need a mediator. Besides, he never went to confessions anyway.

A disturbing realization he'd completely blocked out of his mind struck him. *I have been unfaithful. I cheated on my wife, the love of my life, and the mother of my daughter. How could I have done that?*

Michael reviewed the chain of events that led to his betrayal. He came to the Bishops' estate undercover, pretending to be a lost soul separated from his wife. Perhaps he got too involved in his role-playing? And that was when Mary came on to him? *No! There is no justification for what I've done.* His eyes filled with tears. *Lanie,* without uttering a sound, he cried into the darkness, *please forgive me.*

Feelings of shame and regret engulfed him. Not only had he lied to Bishop and his group, who had welcomed him and accepted him into their community, he'd also cheated on his wife.

He hoped that, upon returning home, his relationship with Melany would return to the harmony they'd always had. On his part, he was going to do whatever he could to make her happy.

Michael was tired. His day started early in the morning, and it would probably continue way past midnight. Although sitting in an uncomfortable position, he fell asleep.

***

When Michael awoke, darkness prevailed—without the penetration of even the tiniest ray of light. He checked his phone and realized that he'd slept nearly an hour. The place was quiet, but after a short while, he heard a distant, muffled sound of a machine working far away. The drill? He pulled the small flashlight from his pocket and turned it on, to avoid tripping over the janitorial equipment stored in the closet. His heart pounded as he exited his hiding place. Using the flashlight to illuminate his way, Michael headed in the direction of the machine. *Who is in there? What will I tell them?* He knew he would have to improvise.

Michael walked down the narrow trail of the Western Wall Tunnels until the path was blocked by a wooden wall. He recognized that he had arrived at the end of the tourist section of the Tunnels. The sound of the machine came from the other side of the barrier. Examining the wood with his flashlight, he perceived a small, almost invisible door. There was no lock or handle on the door, so Michael pushed gently, and it opened. He had to bend to squeeze through the small opening. After passing, Michael paused to calm his breathing, which had become rapid and shallow. It occurred to him that, whether or not he succeeded in his mission, this would be a night he'd never forget.

He continued on a narrow path that appeared like it was newly carved. The air was dusty, and Michael wished he had a mask or an extra cloth to tie around his mouth and nose. Bending and squeezing in sections, and even crawling where the ceiling was very low, he followed the machine's sound as it grew louder. Grasping that he was moving eastward, Michael knew he must already be under the Temple Mount. Adrenaline quickened his heartbeat, enhanced his agility, and sharpened his mind.

The sound of the machine got louder and louder as he advanced under the Temple Mount. There were places where the trail widened into coves, full of large and small rocks and soil. In one of the coves, he saw old fragments of clay pottery and even one whole pot. The vessel was about two feet in height, and several cracks ran through it, but it was otherwise intact. Markings in a language that resembled Hebrew were drawn on the pot's side. Michael remembered the tour guide mentioning the treasures to be found under the Temple Mount.

In some of the coves, Michael saw sacks stacked against the wall. These were not ancient artifacts. Upon examining the sacks, there was no mistake about their content: Semtex, which Michael identified as a powerful plastic explosive. *They're really planning to do it.* He checked his phone—almost 11:00 PM. It was getting close to what Bishop called the zero hour. Pretty soon, a blackout would hit the entire country. Then helicopters would deliver the sections of the temple to be assembled on the Temple Mount. When would they blow up the Dome of the Rock?

He entered a chamber so filled with dusty air he couldn't tell if it was recently carved or it had been there for centuries. The machine made a deafening noise as it ground through layers of tough clay-based soil mixed with the debris of ancient ruins. Three people operated a massive piece of drilling equipment. Illuminated by construction lights, they faced away from him.

This is it. A new rush of energy flooded Michael. *This is* **my** *zero hour. Either I succeed, or it's World War III.*

"Hi! Hello!" he yelled and waved his flashlight. "Stop! I have to talk to you!" *What on earth will I tell them?*

The machine stopped, and Michael breathed a sigh of relief as the unbearable noise turned into silence. The three people wore industrial earplugs and protective eyewear. He knew them all from God's Land: Ron, Roger, and Ruth. Of course, Ruth. Who else would be eager to employ explosives?

"Michael?" They seemed surprised as they took off their eye protection and earplugs. "What are you doing here?"

"I have a message from Charles," he said, trying to look confident as he improvised.

"What kind of message?" Ron asked suspiciously.

"He wants you to stop. He canceled the plan to blow up the Dome of the Rock. He'll build the temple next to it."

"Is this true?" Ron shined a powerful flashlight in Michael's face and examined him.

"It is!" Michael said. "Why don't you call and ask him?"

Michael knew the place had no reception, though if Ron went to the entrance of the Western Wall Tunnels and managed to talk to Charles, his bluff would be exposed. As it was, he was buying himself precious time.

The three of them looked at Michael in disbelief, though they didn't seem to regard him as a spy or traitor. That fact was apparently reserved for the organization's top leaders. If Paul was in that leadership circle, that could explain why he didn't want Michael around.

Ron pulled out his phone. His intention to make the verifying call suggested that, even during the blackout, the group had ways of communicating with each other and receiving instructions from their leaders.

"No signal," Ron grumbled. "I'll go to where there's reception. What Michael says sounds awfully suspicious to me, and I got to get to the bottom of this." He headed toward the trail and paused beside Michael. "You better not lie to us, or you'll end up buried here for the next ten centuries!" and he walked out.

"Michael," Ruth said, "I never heard of Charles changing his mind about anything."

"Ruth," Michael said, "Charles had to make a critical decision, and, after all, he's just human."

"I remember Charles changing his mind," Roger said. "It was before you joined, Ruth, but when we had to decide where on the estate we should build the prototype temple—"

"Okay, guys," Ruth capitulated with a sigh. "I guess we'll wait till Ron comes back. In the meantime, I have to go to the ladies' room. I heard the Romans built some nice bathtubs somewhere around here."

"It's true, Ruth," Michael said. "But it was in a different millennium." Michael took the opportunity to lighten up and pretend he had nothing to worry about.

Ruth disappeared into the darkness.

Roger turned to the machine, opened the lid to the fuel tank, and proceeded to fill the tank from a jerrycan.

I must act now, Michael thought, *I'll never get a better chance.* He seized the opportunity when Roger had his back turned toward him and he was occupied with the fuel, and quickly picked up a medium-size rock that fit the palm of his hand. *I've not been involved in a physical fight since elementary school.* His heart raced as he approached Roger from behind and asked in a casual manner, "do you think that Ruth is a lesbian?"

308

Still focused on the fuel, Roger answered, "It sure looks that way, though I wouldn't—"

Michael slammed the rock into Roger's head, praying that his hit was strong enough to knock Roger unconscious, but not so hard that he caused severe or permanent damage.

Roger collapsed.

I have to prevent this darned world war, Michael justified. He didn't have time to check on Roger's condition, because Ron and Ruth would soon return.

Michael hurried to the corner of the chamber, where he spotted a large pile of debris. He filled his bare hands with as much dust, sand, stones, and little pebbles as he could. He knew that if he dumped the materials into the open fuel tank—it would be enough to jam the machine. He rushed back toward the drill. There was no time to waste.

"Drop it!" Ruth's voice sounded loud and clear, and it echoed in the small chamber.

Michael glanced toward the trail, where she stood, pointing a gun directly at him.

"Drop the sand and move away from the machine," Ruth commanded, "or I swear to God, I'll shoot you."

Michael stood in his place but didn't drop the sand. Less than two yards separated him from the machine. He had no doubt Ruth wasn't bluffing, and she wouldn't hesitate to make good on her threat. Was he ready to sacrifice himself? Be a martyr? Could he leap forward, get shot, and still dump the sand into the fuel tank?

"Michael, I'm done warning you," Ruth said, as she released the weapon's safety.

"Hold it, Ruth!" Ron yelled, storming up the trail.

"Are you crazy?" Ron approached Ruth, glancing at her stance and the firearm in her hands.

"He hit Roger with a rock, and he wants to jam the machine," Ruth said and continued to point the gun at Michael.

"I go for five minutes, and you guys completely flip out," Ron complained. "I talked to Charles, and indeed, he changed his mind about blowing the Dome of the Rock. Michael was telling the truth."

Ruth lowered the gun. Even with the minimal light, Michael could see that she was surprised to hear about him telling the truth. However, he was even more surprised. *Charles changed his mind? He confirmed the conversation we never had?*

Ron approached Roger and emptied a large bottle of water on his head, and then another bottle. Roger opened his eyes and gasped as he moved to a sitting position.

"What happened?" Roger asked and rubbed the bulge at the side of his head.

"I'm sorry," Michael muttered, avoiding Roger's gaze.

"And you," Ron turned toward Michael, narrowing his eyes. "I thought you were a reasonable person. What in Christ's name came over you? Didn't you think I was gonna come back?"

"I don't know," Michael mumbled. "I just thought … you know, Charles said it was important—"

"Let's get out of here," Ron said. "We should go and help our brothers and sisters assemble the temple."

"This place starts to give me the creeps," Ruth said. "It's like some ghost of a dead crusader will walk in on us."

They proceeded toward the door. Michael reached out an arm to help support Roger, but he pushed him away. "Don't you ever get near me again!" Roger snapped, "or you'll wish we left you buried under the Temple Mount."

They made their way out of the newly dug area under the Temple Mount and into the visitor's area of the Western Wall Tunnels.

As they got close to the exit door, Ron grabbed Michael by the arm. His grip was tight and painful.

"Give me your phone," he ordered.

"My phone?"

"Give me your darned phone. I ain't playin' games." Ron tightened his grip.

"Okay." Michael reached for his phone and handed it to Ron.

Ron took the phone and smashed it on the ceramic tile floor. The phone shattered, and fragments of glass scattered the ground.

"And now your flashlight," Ron demanded.

Michael handed him his flashlight without arguing, and Ron smashed it too.

"You stay here!" Ron ordered. "You've caused enough problems, and I don't trust you."

Ron, Ruth, and Roger left the Western Wall Tunnels' site, slamming the doors behind them and leaving Michael locked alone in the dark.

Chapter 46

Groping in the dark, Michael searched for his phone. His eyes tried to adjust, to find something to focus on, but to no avail. Darkness surrounded him, thick, stuffy, and burdensome. *It's the blackout*, he thought, Charles' people are continuing with their plan.

He found his phone, not before sustaining minor cuts to the tips of his fingers from the glass shards of the phone's screen. Slipping the ruined device into his pocket, he didn't even try to turn it on. He figured that, when the electric power resumed, he'd be able to remove the SIM card, and as soon as he got to the city, he'd buy a new phone and return to the twenty-first century.

Fumbling around the dark reception center of the *Western Wall Tunnels*, Michel stumbled upon a chair. He sat down, took a deep breath, and tried to relax his body and mind. Attempting to collect his thoughts, he reflected on the unusual events that had taken place earlier.

If McPherson is right, then I might have saved the world from World War III. An ominous feeling told him that he hadn't prevented the war, only postponed it.

Different thoughts rumbled through his mind. Images of the temple flickered along with those of the Dome of the Rock. Muslims in their traditional garments jumbled with Orthodox Jews, Charles and Mary, Melany and Linda: they all blurred together. As he allowed fatigue to take over, his head dropped forward and he dozed off.

***

Fire raged on the Temple Mount. Michael stood in the Western Wall's square and watched the enormous flames soar up to the heavens. The dark smoke that billowed from the fire covered the entire sky over the city of Jerusalem, and what would have been a bright sunny day had turned into dusk.

Michael attempted to grasp the meaning of the event. He tried to remember how it started, and whether he was somehow connected to it, when suddenly, a massive explosion rocked the ground he stood on, and everything around him shook. Petrified, he stared at the mountain and watched how the Dome of the Rock crack and then collapse,

314

engulfed by the ferocious blaze that rapidly devoured it, reducing it to rubble.

"He did it!" an old Arab woman shrouded in a black burka pointed her finger directly at Michael.

"It wasn't me," he protested. "I just—"

"He did it! He did it!" she shrieked. "Kill him!"

Since she was covered from head to toe, he could only see her eyes, and they conveyed utter hatred and rage.

Much to his horror, he saw horses galloping down from the burning Temple Mount. There was no doubt where their riders were headed.

Michael knew he must escape. He started to run away. If he could make it to the steep stairs that went up to the Jewish quarter, he might save himself. Horses couldn't climb stairs, or could they?

But there was still a long way in front of him and the horsemen, wearing traditional black galabias, waved their swords as they quickly closed the gap, rushing to take revenge upon him. He ran as fast as he could, and he kept pumping his arms and legs even when he was gasping desperately, but the stairs leading to safety never came any closer.

An arrow hit the ground beside him, then another and another, each getting closer and closer. Michael paused for a brief moment and darted a glance at the horsemen who were closing in on him. They yelled, "Allahu Akbar," and he knew he was doomed.

***

"*Adoni, ma ata ose po?*"

"Hmm, what?" It took him a few seconds to realize he was still in the lobby of the *Western Wall Tunnels*.

"*Eich nichnasta lekan?*"

A massive woman was standing in front of him, holding a broom. Clearly the cleaning lady, she glared at him, pointing an accusatory finger at the broken glass.

"Do you speak English?" he asked.

"No English, *ani koret lamishtara*." She had unnaturally blond hair and she spoke Hebrew with a Russian accent.

Michael remembered a few Hebrew words that Ruth had taught him in *God's Land*, and he'd learned a few more words in the past couple of days. It wasn't enough to carry a conversation, but still, he understood that the big woman threatened to call the police.

Bewildered, still trying to separate dreams from reality, both being almost equally inconceivable and bizarre, Michael saw that the front door was wide open.

He got up and made his way out of the *Western Wall Tunnels* and into a cool, sunny morning.

"*Adoni, hake po!*" she yelled after him. "*Ani koret lamishtara!*"

Not having time for unnecessary, tedious explanations, he hurried away.

Hesitantly, he looked in the direction of the Temple Mount. From where he was, right in front of the Western Wall, he saw nothing unusual. The golden cap of the Dome of the Rock gleamed undisturbed. Michael took a deep breath, welcoming the sight.

Walking briskly, he exited the Western Wall's square and made his way to the Temple Mount. If Bishop's people had succeeded in constructing the temple next to the Dome of the Rock, there would be trouble that even the most experienced spokesperson would have a hard time defending.

At the checking post, the armed Israeli soldiers asked if he carried weapons.

"No," he answered impatiently, as he noted that nothing appeared out of the ordinary. He hoped the soldiers wouldn't find him suspicious and waste his time with unnecessary questions.

The Temple Mount appeared serene. Just as it was … just yesterday? It seemed like ages ago. There was no new temple, and he didn't see the commotion he expected.

But that was odd, Michael thought. How could that be? He'd managed to make them abort the more devious plan of blowing up the Dome of the Rock, but he assumed that the project of resurrecting the temple on the Temple Mount would proceed according to plan. They wouldn't have canceled it, would they? They'd put too much time, effort, money, and other resources into that undertaking. Devoted to their mission and to Charles Bishop, they were passionate about creating the right conditions for the return of Christ. Restoring the temple was one of those main conditions …

And then he saw it—the temple. Not the actual temple, but a large photo of it, on the front page of a newspaper that an old Arab man read. He didn't understand the Arabic writing, but the photo was clear and unmistakable.

Where was it? Michael thought it was unlikely that the old man spoke English, and he had no time to waste.

Where was the temple? It must have been somewhere in Jerusalem, and he had to get there. He needed to get there, not because he was a spokesman—that role was clearly behind him—but because … Michael realized that the assignment McPherson handed him had grown beyond what he ever imagined. During the last few months, when the temple became the focal point of his undertaking, he'd become enchanted by the ancient shrine. He felt as though invisible strings connected him to the temple, strange as it may seem.

When Michael thought about the temple, his mind built several temples bundled into one concept: the temple that stood in *God's Land*, which was the only one that he visited; the old temples that stood on the Temple Mount and were destroyed two thousand years ago; and, the new temple, the one Bishop's group concentrated their efforts on resurrecting. Although they were different from one another, the dimensions were near-identical.

Although raised a Christian, Michael was essentially agnostic. However, the temple stirred something within him—a spirit, a sacredness that was missing in his life—and he had Charles Bishop to thank for it.

Three hundred years ago, the concept and the dimensions of the shrine captivated Isaac Newton, who believed it was designed by God. Newton was misunderstood, even ridiculed by his peers. They praised his scientific accomplishments and completely ignored his theological quest; but he had his truth, and he pursued it.

Michael hurried out of the Temple Mount and exited the old city of Jerusalem through the Dung Gate.

Now, where? He assumed that if the temple had been built anywhere in the vicinity of Jerusalem, as he concluded from the newspaper, then all the taxi drivers must know about it.

In a nearby parking lot, Michael spotted a taxi, where the driver leisurely read a newspaper. A glance informed Michael that it was the same Arabic newspaper he saw on the Temple Mount.

"Could you take me there?" Michael asked and pointed to the photo of the temple in the newspaper.

"Ah, the temple, sure," the driver replied in a heavy Arabic accent.

"On the way, please stop at a store where I can buy a new cell phone."

"No problem," the driver said as he drove out of the parking lot.

"You know," the driver said, "It's a good thing they didn't put the temple on the Temple Mount, or there would be war."

"You don't think the Muslims would accept a temple next to the Dome of the Rock?"

"Are you Jewish?" The driver inquired.

"I'm not," Michael replied.

At a red light, the driver examined Michael with a piercing look. "Well, next to our Dome of the Rock? No way!" the driver said. "You know the Jews; sooner or later, they will want to remove the Dome of the Rock, and we can't agree to that. You know that we don't even believe them when they say that the temple used to stand on the Temple Mount?"

"Not even two thousand years ago?" Michael wondered.

"No! You know, the Jews like to make up stories."

"I'm a Christian," Michael said. "We also believe that there was a Jewish temple on the Temple Mount."

"I don't know about the Christians," the driver responded. "We fought against them, but that was a long time ago. You know that as Muslims, we believe in Jesus? He is one of the greatest prophets in Islam, but not as great as Muhammad."

The driver pulled into a parking lot of an electronics store. Michael hopped out of the car and into the store. He didn't spend much time shopping but picked the first phone that grabbed his attention.

"Could you transfer the SIM from my old phone?" he asked the clerk who appeared eager to help.

"Sure," the seller said, and within a short time, Michael was out of the store with a new phone.

"Where are you from?" The taxi driver asked when they continued on their way.

"New York."

"I have a brother who is a doctor in New York," the driver said proudly. "He got tired of the turmoil in the Middle East."

"And you?" Michael asked.

"I lived here all my life, and I love this city with all its problems."

Michael nodded and checked his new phone. It appeared the battery was partially charged, and the SIM card retained all the contacts. *It could have been worse.*

"I think," the driver said, "that it's a good thing they built the temple next to the Israel Museum, though I don't know how they did it in one night, whoever they were."

"You mean the temple is next to the museum?" Michael was surprised.

"Yes, and it's a good place for it. Now they have their place, and we have ours."

The streets in the vicinity of the museum were jammed, and the taxi barely moved. So, Michael paid the driver and thanked him. He stepped out of the taxi and hurried in the direction the driver guided him.

Once in front of the museum and temple, Michael gawked, immediately stricken by the magnificent structure. No matter how many times he'd seen the temple, it never failed to amaze him.

Chapter 47

*And I saw the holy city, new Jerusalem, coming down from God out
of heaven, prepared as a bride adorned for her husband.*

- The Book of Revelation

News traveled fast. It was still morning when Michael arrived
at the Israel Museum. The temple, which materialized near the
Institution, drew large crowds of spectators from all walks of
life who gathered to see the wonder. Children with their
parents or teachers. Teenage girls with revealing clothes and
piercings stood next to religious Jews in their black outfits and
long beards. Even Arabs from the Muslim quarter of the old
city and Christians from the Armenian quarter came to
examine the new marvel.

Michael was familiar with what went on behind the scenes
of the temple's construction. He knew about Bishop and his
devoted group investing months, even years, in planning and

preparations, including the building of a prototype model. He knew about them adhering to Newton's measurements and how they revered their work and viewed it as their sacred duty. He knew about the use of helicopters in delivering different sections in order to assemble them on site.

But for the people who now gazed at a finished creation that had sprung up overnight, Michael could tell that it was nothing short of a miracle.

Michael passed near a television crew who interviewed a distinguished professor: "... no matter how secular we've become, we'll always have the temple wired into our DNA ..." He continued walking around the gigantic structure and couldn't help but admire Bishop's people for the great endeavor.

He saw a group of Orthodox Jews. Some prayed facing the temple, but most appeared perplexed, not knowing how to deal with the new situation. Conversing with each other in low voices, they waited for leading rabbis to issue a decree telling them what to think and how to behave.

Not far from the Orthodox men stood a group of Orthodox women in their modest outfits. The women maintained a distance from the men so as not to violate the rules of decency.

Screaming children, clothed according to strict Orthodox rules, chased each other around the women.

One woman separated from the pack. Like the rest of them, her hair was wrapped in a coif. She pushed a baby stroller and advanced in Michael's direction.

"Quite a scene," she remarked in English.

Her voice sounded familiar. Michael looked into her playful green eyes. "Rachel?" He let out a laugh. "You truly are a chameleon."

"I told you I'm an actress." She smiled.

"And who's the cute baby?"

"This is David, one of my sister's kids," she replied. For a moment, she looked around, observing the temple, "Quite strange that they ended up building it here and not on the Temple Mount."

"I just came from the Temple Mount," Michael said. "I expected to find it there."

"I think that here, it's not gonna cause any problem," she said and examined the growing crowd.

"My Arab taxi driver approved this location," Michael smiled.

Rachel's phone rang and she answered it. "Hello … yes, it's me … I'm standing right in front of it … it looks incredible … Michael happens to be here with me."

She handed Michael the phone. "Stewart wants to talk to you."

"Hi, Stewart," Michael said.

"And how is my hero doing?" McPherson asked.

"Tired, and also trying to figure out why the temple wound up next to the museum and not on the Temple Mount."

"It's there because the group is very disciplined," McPherson replied, "and they did what Charles Bishop told them."

"Do you know why Bishop changed his mind?" Michael rubbed his crinkled forehead.

"He didn't," McPherson said. "It was me. I instructed them about the change of a plan."

"You did?" Michael was puzzled.

"Yes. Though I used Charles Bishop's voice. You see, Irene and Alex worked on a sophisticated algorithm. They sampled all the lectures that you recorded, words, phrases, even single syllables, and created a large pool of data. When I spoke, the program substituted my words with Bishop's, recorded in his own, natural voice. Obviously, we couldn't have done it without you getting us the recordings."

"How long did you have that capability?" Michael inquired.

"Actually, it was down to the wire. These last few days, Irene and the other members of the team got very little sleep as they worked around the clock."

"So, Stewart," Michael suddenly understood, "when Ron came and said that Charles confirmed what I said—"

"That was me, of course," McPherson confirmed.

Michael remembered how Ruth was surprised when Ron corroborated his claim about Charles changing his mind. He remembered that he'd been even more surprised than she.

"And may I ask how you took over their computer systems? I mean, you had the algorithm or whatever it was to talk in Charles' voice, but how did you go about receiving the call in the first place?"

"You see," McPherson answered patiently, "even the most protected systems need to leave a back door open for their programmers, and of course, for their people when they are away. For that purpose, the systems are usually protected by passwords. A password can be replaced every so often, but still, it's usually something that a person can remember, like a

328

birth date, a spouse's name, kid's names, etc. In the case of Bishop's people, we had an advantage because we knew they would want to align themselves with biblical prophecies and with their mission, so it had to be related either to the temple, to the Book of Revelation, to Isaac Newton, and so on. We fed all the possible choices into a hacking program that John, my hacker, brought. Our most valuable resource in this password guesswork was the information that you provided when you infiltrated their computer center.

"I hope you know that I didn't want to do that," Michael said.

"Believe it or not," McPherson said, "I didn't like sending you on that particular mission. I'm grateful it worked out, and of course, it proved tremendously valuable."

"Sounds like we beat them in their own game."

"We sure did," McPherson agreed.

"You know, Stewart," Michael said, "there are still large amounts of explosives stashed under the Temple Mount. I'm going to inform the Israeli authorities, so they can remove it."

"Do that, and then come home," McPherson said, "I assume you're relieved of your duty as the group's spokesman."

"I'm relieved of all my duties with the group. They will probably never want to see me or hear my name again."

"Michael," McPherson said, seeming to detect some sadness in the younger man's voice, "a lot of people all over the world owe you a huge debt, even if they don't know it."

"And I just want to go home to be with my family," Michael replied.

Chapter 48

Michael took a taxi to Jerusalem's central police department, where he informed the startled policemen that large amounts of explosives were deposited under the Dome of the Rock. The Israeli officials treated his report with the utmost seriousness and subjected Michael to an intense investigation by special security service agents.

"What's your involvement with the group?"

"What were the group's objectives?"

"Who is the leader of the group?"

"Who is *your* superior?"

"Why didn't you come forward earlier?"

"Are you aware of the severity of your actions?"

"Are you still in contact with the group?"

"Were there Israeli collaborators?"

On and on, the questions continued and repeated themselves. Michael tried to answer the queries patiently and earnestly.

"I have nothing to hide," he kept saying. And, "No, I don't need a lawyer."

After hours of interrogation, Michael was finally free to go.

Discreetly and safely, an Israeli bomb squad unit removed the explosives from under the Temple Mount, and they sealed the tunnel Bishop's people had dug with cement.

All members of Bishop's group left Israel in a hurry before the Israeli officials could detain and question them. Still, Israel notified American authorities of the dangerous and illegal activities conducted by American citizens.

Several media channels received a short message generated by a source located in the State of Washington. The announcement that claimed responsibility for resurrecting the Holy Temple was signed by a man named Charles Bishop. He identified himself as a devout Christian and a follower of Jesus Christ. Bishop asserted that the temple had been constructed with strict adherence to the design and measurements of Sir Isaac Newton, based on writings from the Old Testament. Bishop extended his wish for peace on earth to prevail for all time.

After purchasing his ticket back to the United States, Michael spent the night at a hotel in Tel Aviv. He felt the need to get away from Jerusalem, where the complex religious history weighed upon him.

Early in the morning, he went for a long walk on the beach, enjoying the sounds of the surf and sea birds, relishing the scenery, the merging of the blue sea and sky over the horizons, and reflecting on the recent events.

Michael didn't eat much of the hotel's generous Mediterranean breakfast. After packing his belongings, he took a shuttle to Ben Gurion Airport, where he was required to check in three hours before the flight. While sitting and waiting for the long flight home, his new phone rang.

"Hello, Michael." Mary's deep, warm voice sent a tingle down his spine.

"Mary," he said after a stunned second, "I'm so sorry for not being honest with you and Charles. I—"

"Michael," she interrupted, "why don't you calm down and listen to what I have to say!"

"I'm listening," he said and took a deep breath.

"We knew about you," Mary said. "Charles suspected you were a spy on the day you arrived. Your request for permission to record his lectures convinced him. We also saw you in Olympia, where you met regularly with a blonde woman who happens to be a PI. There's a hidden camera in that café. Still, Charles decided not to inform the other group members."

"I don't understand," Michael said. "Why didn't he kick me out, instead of allowing me to stay with the community for more than two months, especially since he suspected I was a spy?"

"I can tell that you still don't know Charles," she said. "You see, Charles is a true believer: he trusts God, and believes that God is the creator of the world, and that everything has a reason. In that respect, you, too, were sent to us by God. Charles recognized you as a kindred soul who could become a true believer. Michael, it's no accident that you arrived here. If you took an honest look at your life, you would realize that coming here was one of the most wonderful things to ever happen to you. You met Charles, a most beautiful person, guided by compassion, not ambition. He still loves you, and nothing can change that. He loves you as you are, and not because you're doing one thing or another."

"But I intervened in his plan and prevented the construction of the temple on the Temple Mount."

"Charles, and I, too, see the mission as a monumental success. Although the temple was not constructed on the Temple Mount, it *is* standing in Jerusalem for the first time in two thousand years, and it's receiving worldwide attention. By now, all the major TV news networks have covered the story. Protestants and Catholics alike, not to mention most Jews, are treating it as a miracle. So, we're quite confident that the Israeli government will not take it down. This outcome is not what we envisioned, but it's the will of the Lord, and we have to accept it humbly. We were willing to follow our Lord's plan no matter what consequences it would bring, including Armageddon, but now that a world war was averted, we naturally feel relieved. We are not warmongers."

"You're relieved that your plan didn't fully succeed?"

"Michael, at the time, we believed that to fulfill the prophecies outlined in the Book of Revelations and other sources, the Temple Mount was the only location for the temple's resurrection. However, we treated our mission with a heavy heart, being fully aware of the tragic consequences that would ensue. As it turned out, your intervention actually provided an unpredicted solution that we accept as the will of the good Lord."

"Did the U.S. authorities contact you?" he asked.

"Not yet, and we're not concerned about it. So far, we've only been approached by the major TV networks who wish to interview Charles."

"And the other people on *God's Land*? Don't they wish that Charles had kicked me out? Don't they ask why he didn't?"

"Michael," Mary said, "I could ask you a similar question. You want to know why Charles didn't kick you out, and I'm asking, why didn't you turn us in? Why didn't you approach the FBI or the Israeli police and inform them of our covert activities *before* the temple was built?"

The question caught him off-guard. Why hadn't he? Really?

"I guess," he said, "it sounded quite far-fetched, and I didn't think they would believe me. Besides, I didn't know about the plan to blow up the Dome of the Rock, and I thought—"

"Oh, come on," she dismissed his attempt. "From *you*, I would expect a more sincere answer. You know very well that even if they didn't trust your information, they would have

336

had to check its validity. No! The reason why you didn't turn on us is that during the time you'd spent with us, you saw that we're not a group of crazy fanatics as you were probably led to believe. You became sympathetic to our cause. I would even venture to say that, deep inside, you became a believer, although you don't know it yet."

Michael noted that she spoke fervently and with deep conviction.

"Does Charles know about ..." Michael hesitated, "... about us?"

"He does. He knows that I love him dearly, and he's the only man that matters in my life. But as I told you, I am not a Madonna, I'm a mature woman and I have a woman's needs."

"Is he angry with me?"

"No. I told him the truth, which is that I seduced you. Michael, I know you tried hard to resist me, but you never stood a chance. My advice to you is: don't tell your wife what happened; it will needlessly complicate things between the two of you. As I see it, you got swept away while being on an assignment, and in your mind, you didn't really betray her."

"No, Mary!" Michael said. "I don't agree with you at all. I *did* betray my wife, the precious woman I share my life with. Whether I tell her or not, *I* will have to live with the consequences. I will *always* have to compensate her for my actions."

An announcer called passengers to board his flight. "Mary, I have to go now."

"Goodbye, Michael."

"Goodbye."

Chapter 49

Melany

Michael is coming home!

Linda is so happy and excited; she can't wait and she's a bit hyper, but I understand and I'm patient with her. As much as this ordeal has been difficult for me, I recognize that it was much harder on her—having her beloved daddy suddenly disappearing from her life. I'm sure no matter how much we've tried to reassure her that this was a temporary phase, deep inside, she felt scared and abandoned. Throughout this time, I tried to be forgiving with her—when she misbehaved—but I recognize that there were times when I snapped.

Me, I have mixed feelings. Naturally, I'm thrilled and relieved my husband is returning to me; but I doubt we could continue as if nothing had happened. It was an intense time for Linda and me. We went through changes, and I'm sure Michael did too.

I remember that Michael said he wouldn't go if I hadn't let him. So, I told him to go—do what he had to, and come back to his family. However, after he left, I wondered why he needed this break from us in the first place. Wasn't he happy with his life with Linda and me? Didn't he know how much we love him?

I hardly know anything about Michael's life when he was with the cult, and for some reason, I have a bad feeling about it. It's just a hunch, or a woman's intuition, however, I can't shake off the suspicion that Michael had been unfaithful. Perhaps it's all in my head, God, I hope it is. I have too much time to think about all kinds of weird scenarios, and it drives me crazy. If he cheated on me, would I want to know about it? Strangely, the answer is a resounding *no*!

Perhaps I'm just hurt because even if there was no other woman, he still left me. He preferred McPherson and the cult over his family. It's possible that I'm just narrow-minded, and it will turn out that he really went to save the world.

I know time heals everything, and I hope we'll get through whatever problems may arise, and come out stronger.

Now I have to go and pick Linda from school, and then we'll drive to the airport.

Chapter 50 - Epilogue

Fifty Years Later

An old man traveled from the United States to Jerusalem.

His original intention was to go alone and make it a journey of contemplation and reflection. However, his beloved granddaughter, Tammy, had asked if she could join him, and he couldn't refuse her.

"But you are not a religious man, Grandpa," she said.

"Indeed, I'm not," he replied, smiling at her lovingly. "But still, a journey to Jerusalem is somewhat of a religious pilgrimage—or closure—for me."

They arrived in Jerusalem at night and checked into a hotel not far from the city's center. On the following morning, they took a cab, instructing the driver to take them to what had become known as "the new temple," even though it was no longer new.

They joined a group of five tourists who had signed up for a guided tour with an English-speaking tour guide. Speaking with an American accent, a young, friendly, female guide led the small group.

"These days," she explained, "we commemorate fifty years since this temple was created. However, the Orthodox Jewish establishment only made it fully operational about ten years ago after the earthquake that demolished the Temple Mount along with its structures. Before that event, they'd regarded this temple as somewhat of an abomination because it was created by devout Christians and not by Jews. After the earthquake—which they viewed as an act of God—they looked at its miraculous creation and had a change of heart.

"Today, it serves as Israel's most treasured synagogue, where the country's most important religious ceremonies are held, though they are still careful not to call it 'The Third Temple.'"

"You mentioned something about a Miraculous Creation," the old man's granddaughter asked. "Could you please elaborate? I mean, what was miraculous about it?"

"Sure," said the tour guide. "For one thing, it was built in one night, which is an incredible achievement."

The tour group participants observed the massive structure. They all shook their heads in disbelief, except for the old American.

"The people of Jerusalem woke up one morning," she continued, "and it was here. Of course, it didn't just descend from the sky, as some wanted to believe. A lot of planning and hard work had gone into it. We know, for instance, that they used powerful military helicopters to transport the separate parts which were assembled in this location. As you can imagine, seeing it the following day was quite a spectacle. It was *as if* it had materialized overnight."

"What was the intended purpose of that elaborate undertaking?" asked one of the participants. He was a tall man who spoke with a German accent.

"The Christian group strived to set the foundations and the right environment for the second coming of Christ," the tour guide responded.

"So did Jesus ever return?" Tammy asked, smiling.

"Some scholars," the tour guide explained somberly, "believe that the second coming should not be viewed literally but as a metaphor for the state of our world. So, if we consider that we essentially live in an era of peace, one could conclude that the second coming has, in fact, happened.

However, note that the leader of the Christian group intended to construct the temple on the Temple Mount, which was known as an extremely volatile location. But somehow

344

the plan was diverted—fortunately, I should say. If they'd followed through with their original idea, the temple would have been destroyed in the earthquake, not to mention the horrible violence that would have been instigated all over the world."

"Is it true," an elderly lady asked, "that the blueprint, the design of the temple, was created by Sir Isaac Newton?"

"That is true," the guide answered. "We know that the great Isaac Newton had thoroughly studied the Old Testament and drew his measurements from the scriptures. So, we can conclude that the temple's design came right out of the Bible. And on the subject of Newton, it is interesting to note that the earthquake that destroyed the Temple Mount occurred in 2060. According to Newton's calculations and prediction, the end of the world would have transpired in that year."

"Was the earthquake that demolished the temple mount a unique event in the history of Israel and Jerusalem?" Asked the elderly lady.

"Not at all," the guide answered. "There is plenty of evidence and documentation of earthquakes that had struck this land for thousands of years. Some quakes are mentioned in the bible—old and new testaments.

"Do you know how the plan to construct the temple on the temple mount was sabotaged?" Tammy's grandfather asked with a small smile.

He reflected on that day, so many years ago, when he'd still been a young man. He remembered entering the Western Wall Tunnels, determined to prevent the plan to blow up the Dome of the Rock, no matter what.

He also remembered his weakest moment during the time he'd stayed with the group, when he'd surrendered to his desires. He never discussed that incident with his wife, but she knew. He knew that she knew. She was hurt, and he saw it in her eyes.

For several months, she'd kept a cold distance between them, and he'd agonized, deeply regretting letting her down. Then, apparently, she'd decided to forgive him and give him another chance. After which, he'd spent the rest of their life together trying his best to make amends.

"This part is still shrouded in mystery," the tour guide answered. "We know that Stewart McPherson, a renowned American journalist, was involved. He feared—and rightfully so—that constructing the temple on the Temple Mount would

346

set the stage for World War III. It would have been a massive clash of civilizations that could have brought the world to the brink of an Apocalypse."

Tammy was familiar with the name Stewart McPherson and knew her grandfather had worked with the esteemed journalist. But she'd never heard about work they may have done in Jerusalem. Now, filled with a new sense of respect, she stared at her grandfather, who seemed to focus on the tour guide's explanations.

"Do you agree with McPherson's assumption that such an action could have caused the Apocalypse?" the German tourist asked.

"Well, thankfully, that is a hypothetical question," said the guide. "It would have certainly brought about a wave of rage and uproar throughout the Muslim world, so we have McPherson to thank for averting the tragedy that would almost certainly have ensued. Obviously," she continued, "we owe a great deal not only to McPherson but also to his dedicated team and particularly to his protégé, who risked his life when he confronted the group. However, McPherson refused to reveal his name, and he remains unknown to this day."

Once again, Tammy felt compelled to turn her head and examine her grandfather. However, his facial expression remained still, and whatever emotions he might have had, he kept to himself.

Standing in front of the magnificent structure, Michael was filled with a deep sense of fulfillment. He did not doubt that if called, he would have done it all over again.

Acknowledgements

I wish to thank Deserae Hunter for the wonderful creative editing.

Thank you, Karen M. Smith, for the meticulous editing, and for contributing to the consistency and coherency of the text.

A special thank you to Terry Hayman, my developmental editor for the helpful comments.

Thank you, Amanda Safran and Melissa Hollingsworth, for the proofreading.

Many thanks to the readers of the manuscript at the various stages for your support and enlightening remarks. Creselinda Porat, Raul Colodner, Anna Elazar, Josef Porat, Mark Bunyard, Ofer Elrom, Jonathan Tzachor, Ella Gafni, and Frank Shaver.

Thank you, Ravi of R-Design and Alon Lubenfeld for the wonderful cover design.

And Linda, for your support, patience, and love.

Thank you all,

Liam Fialkov

Bibliography

- Flynn, David. *Temple at the Center of Time, 2008.*
- Newton, Isaac. *The Mathematical Principles of Natural Philosophy,*1687.
- Newton, Isaac. *The Chronology of Ancient Kingdoms Amended,* 1728.
- Newton, Isaac. *Observations upon the Prophecies of Daniel, and the Apocalypse of St. John,* 1733.
- The Newton Project - newtonproject@history.ox.ac.uk
- Chambers, John. *The Metaphysical World of Isaac Newton,* 2018.
- Morrison, Tessa. *Isaac Newton and the Temple of Solomon,* 2010.
- Wikipedia
- The Bible

If you enjoyed reading *The Newton Code*, it'd be greatly appreciated if you leave a review on Amazon.

https://www.amazon.com/Newton-Code-Mystery-Thriller-ebook/dp/B081944NXF/ref=tmm_kin_swatch_0?_encoding=UTF8&qid=1576058854&sr=1-1

liam_fialkov@outlook.com
https://www.facebook.com/liam.fialkov.77

The author on the Temple Mount, in front of the
Dome of the Rock, and next to the Dome of the Spirits.

The Australian shearer who torched Al Aqsa Mosque in a bid to bring on the apocalypse

ABC Radio National / By Joey Watson and Stan Correy for Late Night Live
Posted Fri 23 Aug 2019 at 11:30pm, updated Sat 24 Aug 2019 at 1:32am

Fifty years ago, a young shearer travelled from Australia to Israel to orchestrate a plot he believed would prompt the return of Jesus Christ and usher in the end of the world.

Denis Michael Rohan started a fire which seriously damaged Jerusalem's Al Aqsa mosque — one of Islam's holiest sites — and shook a region already shrouded in tension.

Many Muslims believed the attack had been orchestrated by Israel, and protests erupted across the Middle East.

"[He believed] that destroying the existing Islamic shrines and replacing them with a temple would have brought about the advent of Jesus Christ." Dr Aldrovandi says.

Rohan was arrested the day after the fire at a kibbutz north of Tel Aviv, where he'd been learning Hebrew since his arrival in Israel. He told police his study of the Bible had convinced him that God wanted him to destroy the mosque.

At his trial he said he was trying to hasten the return of Jesus Christ, fulfilling the will of God communicated to him through the Bible.

"God told me that because I have obeyed him, I will be lifted up above the Earth and God shall bring all the maidens of Israel to me to bear offspring to God's glory," he told the court.[4]

---

[4] *The Newton Code* is a work of fiction; however, it is not without a troubling factual basis. Similar plans to the one portrayed in this novel were carried out ever since Israel captured the Temple Mount in the Six-Day War. In my recent visit to Jerusalem, I sensed how volatile the situation is. I respect true believers of all faiths, and yet, I hope this book serves as a warning to ensure that fanatics—who plot religious wars—will fail to accomplish their wicked goals.

- *Liam Fialkov*